Mary Woronov is an actress turned cult queen thanks to films like *Chelsea Girls*, *Eating Raoul*, and *The Living End*. She is also a painter and the author of three books; a fictional memoir, *Swimming Underground*, a book of LA short stories that illustrated her paintings, *Wake for the Angels*, and a novel *Snake*. She has written five scripts, three of which have been optioned. In order to pay the rent she had to write and direct soft porn for television, and she fell in love with directing.

Swimming Underground and *Snake* are published by Serpent's Tail.

Also by Mary Woronov and published by
Serpent's Tail

Snake: A Novel
Swimming Underground: My Years in the
Warhol Factory

Niagara

Mary Woronov

Library of Congress Catalog Card Number: 2001098635

A complete catalogue record for this book can be
obtained from the British Library on request

First published in 2002 by
Serpent's Tail,
4 Blackstock Mews, London N4 2BT
website: www.serpentstail.com

Typeset by Intype London Ltd
Printed in Great Britain by Mackays of Chatham, plc

10 9 8 7 6 5 4 3 2 1

Contents

For my brother,
Victor D. Woronov, Jr.

1

Inside the Christmas tree

❧

I STARTED DRINKING in the day, and by the time I got to the supermarket I was so loaded I needed a cart to stand up. I like the supermarket. I'm especially satisfied with the order in which everything is kept. It's so controlled. There are borders and designated sectors and entry doors with electric eyes. Inside I feel safe. Yes, yes, yes, pushing the iron wagon in the wonderful rat maze of commercial food. Now, let's see, past the evil red cannibal cow meat, and left at the ochre yellow chicken segments, I score a box of Mallowmars, narrowly missing contact with a slab of toxic fish. All right, good show. We are happy while we push. Outside our sister bag women push the heavy duty shit, and we don't want to be told to go out there and join them. No, no, no, we want to stay in here where it's clean and neat, like Disneyland. It might be the land of a thousand commercials, but it's still Mickey Mouse compared to our grim sisters outside. We are thankful. Somewhere among the canned peas and the sliced Wonder bread I have a thankful attack – I get down on my hands and knees and start whispering, "Mayonnaise, mayonnaise, mayonnaise."

"Can I help you find something, Ma'am?" A Mouse-kateer has spotted me.

"No, no, Mister Mouse, I've got it. It's right here." I pull out the symbol of our nation, Wonder bread. I try not to squeeze it, but I want to. Thank God for these new indestructible wrappers. Before putting it back on the shelf, I have a frenzied squeezing attack.

Okay, I've been here half an hour and all I have is Mallowmars. Hmm, don't want to overstay my welcome. Perhaps it's time to leave. I pick up some other stuff so the Mallowmars won't feel lonely.

There are cameras and mirrors watching us every-where. I fix my hair and try not to look too drunk. At the checkout stand we line up on the border of sanity holding our passports, our visa cards. Some women will make it. Others will be asked to stay with their carts, they will be given different clothes, lobotomies, and schizophrenic outbursts, until they look like they grew out of the pavement without mothers or fathers. A number will be tattooed on their neck and they will be ushered outside through special doors that never let you back in.

"Paper or plastic, ma'am?"

That same cryptic question. I don't know. I think hard. What's the fucking difference? I decide to tell the truth, "Actually, I'd be delighted if you would expose yourself to me. Nothing sexual, of course, I just think you're related to Minnie Mouse, and I want to see the fur on your tummy, the long pink tail folded up in your underwear." I can't help giggling.

An alarm goes off, and people move away from me. The head mouse appears; his chest sign reads "manager." I'm asked to leave. "Can I keep my Mallow-mars, please?" Dumping the required amount of cash on the counter, I smile my best smile and keep it plastered on my face until I'm safely in my car. But where is my car? I can't remember where I parked. I can't even remember who I am. My act, my smile, everything starts to unravel. I panic. I'm having a black-out.

While the parking lot shimmers in the sunlight, I stand there, feeling like someone lost on the Sahara, waiting for the return of my mind. But nothing comes. No little caravan of thoughts, no camel bearing the smallest idea disturbs the glaring emptiness. Inside the memory bank, there has been a power failure. Nothing is working. All the screens are blank. How am I supposed to remember who I am if I can't access my past? Finally a blur comes on screen. Like a white ghost it settles and clings to everything. It's fog, shrouding the looming mountains in a misty white silence so that they vanish and yet you can tell they are still there, perhaps even closer than they were before, because you are moving quickly through time instead of space.

I waited, but all I could see was blue fog everywhere so that I thought I must be drifting on the ocean in the early morning, not that I had ever seen the ocean, but I knew pretty much what it should look like. Squinting hard I could barely make out an island as flat as a table. On it a fire, pale as a lamp, glowed and around it strange beasts crouched and shivered. In their midst, a beautiful

Chinese woman sat still as stone. With a flood of pleasure I realized the woman was my mother dressed in a red silk Chinese dress with gold embroidered dragons on it, wearing make-up that turned her face into a mysterious doll-like mask. By the time I recognized her, the blue fog had turned into the familiar smoke of a gambling room. The beasts became men in crumpled suits, sweat-stained shirts, and loosened ties hunched over their cards and twisting in their chairs. My mother's dress and make-up was always perfect, her body motionless, except for her hands as they turned the cards. Her eyes half closed in pleasure, as the other gamblers growled and grunted before her. Although her mouth was smiling it looked cruel, like the mouth of a wolf as it stands, one paw on its fresh kill, ready to eat. It was the only mouth at the table painted red, and it was victorious.

I know this memory; it's my favorite childhood memory. It's the Garden of Eden that I was thrown out of. I groan to myself. Must I go through my entire life before I remember who I am? Couldn't I start a little later, like yesterday? But no, back to the beginning when Ma was forced to take me with her from one smoky room to another. I didn't mind. On the contrary, I loved being carried on her back close to her. When we arrived she would arrange a nest to put me down in, then she would give me a little Chinese chocolate and a haze of pleasure would descend on me as I watched her drift away on her magical island. In my smoky dreams the embroidered dragon jumped around inside my mother, a fierce demon behind her immobile porcelain face.

After they built the casinos, we went there night after

night. It didn't matter if it was raining or if freezing snow covered the land, a big black car would come out of nowhere to pick us up and take us there. I loved the casino. It was like being inside a Christmas tree with all the lights on. Since children were not allowed on the casino floor my mother and I were immediately ushered into a special room, where under sleepy eyelids I watched Ma transform herself from a little Chinese housewife into a formidable gambler with a reputation that brought people from far away cities like Chicago and Miami.

These were the only times I saw her dressed in old Chinese style: her smooth black hair intricately arranged and held in place with gold sticks, and lucky gold coins gleaming on her ears. At first she was self-effacing, bowing during the introductions, keeping her eyes lowered. Once she took her place on the special satin pillow she brought, she was no longer short. She looked down as her red lips smiled coquettishly, and her equally red nails wrapped around her cards. Slyly she watched the cards as if they were secrets being passed from one man to another, each one having a personal and sexual meaning. Not used to seeing my mother in make-up I was fascinated by her face. It was an alluring face that was aware of its own beauty and promised sexual pleasure, while she was only interested in money. Now she turned that face on her opponents like a radar dish scanning for information. Her eyes, no longer lowered, flirted openly over the tops of her cards, not with the other players, but with their cards, with chance, and loss, and death, the chance that they might win, might escape death even as their youth slipped from their fingers. She was hypnotic, and she knew it.

I am not sure, but I think Ma drugged me with those chocolates because I would always fall asleep at this point no matter how much I tried to keep my eyes on her. Hours later I would wake up in the same room to find it filled with blue smoke. As soon as Ma saw I was awake she would end the game, which made the other animals growl and bark. Once I saw a man cry and grab her hand, pleading for another game but we left anyway. As she pulled her hand out of his, her eyes glittered and her red lips broke into a rare tinkling laugh of pleasure.

Leaving was my favorite part of this nocturnal voyage. That's when the same man with the long black hair came to pick me up in his arms and carry me through the casino as if I was on a boat sailing through a kaleidoscope of music and lights. On the main floor heads looked up from their cards and dice and cease-lessly turning roulette wheels as we followed Ma across the casino floor. I always felt sorry for these people because they were never allowed to leave. When we came back, it seemed to me, those same people were still there doing the same things over and over.

The man carrying me smelled of trees after a heavy rain. He was very tall and dark, and he always called me princess. When he said good night, he would look me in the eye and say "promise me you'll take care of your mother and protect her from the hungry river spirits."

Take care of my mother indeed. How could I take care of her? I was too small. All I could do was worry about her. I checked on her constantly. But sometimes she disappeared into her room in the middle of the day. Other times she wouldn't come out of her room until dinner. I would hang around her door in an anxious frenzy until I was shooed away. Then I would have to sneak back to check and make sure she was still in there and not being eaten by some hungry spirit that could walk through walls and had bad breath and teeth the size of carving knives.

And was she at all grateful to the little soldier who stood guard at her door? No. Instead of gratitude she stopped taking me up river to the casino with her. I was left at home like a bag of laundry. Every time she dressed to leave I would grab the hem of her scarlet dress and leave wet tear marks on it. I wouldn't get up off my knees; I begged her to take me, just like that gambler had begged her for one last game, and still she left without me. I was miserable. I couldn't understand what I had done to be so suddenly excluded. Her response was cold and without emotion, "You're too old to go, too old to cry. You have school work now."

She had never used that tone with me before. It was as if I had crossed some invisible line and, unable to crawl back under the blanket of her protection, I was left on the outside where her voice was cold and her look was hard. And if growing up meant nothing more than losing what you prized most, then I had nothing to look forward to.

School was like a prison sentence. No more trips to the inside of the Christmas tree to see the beasts of men sit in a circle with Ma, her red nails and red mouth glowing like danger beacons in the tobacco fog. Never again would the tall dark man with the long black hair carry me to the waiting car. No, I had to sit home like a prisoner in a cave, reading about how Dick and Jane and Spot ran up the hill. If only the trees living on that hill would rip them to shreds and throw them in the river along with their golden leaves, I would be very happy.

2

Dr Ming

OF COURSE, NOW that the lights are up and running in the memory bank, memories start popping up all over the place. This is why I drink, to get rid of these annoying fragments of my past. But as I stand here helpless in a parking lot, they descend on me like a cloud of black flies: the agony of beginning school, of being left out, of being left at home, of being alone.

Another memory buzzes around me. This one is only a sound but it is as familiar as my heartbeat. It's the sound of Niagara. We lived so close to the Falls that the sound of it was always there waiting for me. It filled the empty rooms of my childhood so that I was not afraid of being left alone when Ma hung the lucky gold coins on her ears and I knew she was going to the casino without me.

The worst part about being left at home was that I couldn't sleep without the little Chinese chocolates. Instead of dreams, I twisted and flopped around on my bed like a fish on the bottom of the boat that can feel the river is near but can't get to it. It was only by concentrating on the sound of Niagara that I could glide into the river again and finally drift away into sleep.

Niagara could speak the secret language of children; "Hush, hush, those are not the hungry river spirits coming to eat your hair and fingers and bones. All those shadows on the walls are only clouds that can't get off the earth. Do not be afraid of them. They are sad, waiting for the day they will be set free."

"But when is that? I've never seen a world without shadows."

"When my princess is given back to me," the voice of the Falls would whisper. "The shadows will be set free and there will be no more tears." Then the roar of the Falls bemoaned its loss and we would cry together, him for his princess and me for the woman who used to be my mother. And then, I think, grow up already. I was really crying for myself because, like all the princesses in my fairy tales, I was convinced I had a mother who was cold and cruel.

Okay, enough of this shit. I remember who I am. I'm a Chinese-American female standing in a parking lot. Thank God that's cleared up. Now, where the fuck is my car? But it's not cleared up. I have to remember more, like my name, Mei Li. No, my name is Molly, Molly Carson. Only Ma called me Mei Li, usually when she was angry with me and it seems she was always angry. My slightest error, and there were many of them according to her, would make her yell at me.

If I did anything wrong she yelled and if I pleased her, she ignored it as if I were in danger of becoming swellheaded. Soon, even if I didn't disobey her she screamed at me. Did she think that all young people were deaf? Or was it that she was so short she had to make up for it in vocal capacity? I wanted to talk to her, but rather than communicating the nest of insecurities she slept with every night, she didn't communicate at all. Instead she tried to intimidate me. I retaliated by stuffing cotton in my ears. If she pushed me away so I would not grow up like her, and cried at night because she no longer had a daughter, I didn't hear it.

She was impossible to love and even harder to hate. I couldn't figure her out. There were times when I thought she loved me deeper than anything in the universe – like the time in the back yard when fat Bobby Earlanger told me to hold still while he shot things off the top of my head with his new sling shot gun. In her haste to stop him, Ma jumped out of the first-story window instead of using the door. She chased him all the way to his house. I tried to tell her the only reason I played with Bobby was because we were both playground rejects, me because I was Asian and Bobby because he was fat. He was going up the stairs just as Ma's hand closed over his ankle. With the fierceness of a terrier pulling a rat out of its hole, she pulled him all the way down the stairs while he tried to climb back up, grabbing the banister and screaming for his uncle. She yelled at his uncle too, when he came out in his undershirt, dismay scribbled all over his face, and when she was finished, Mr Earlanger took away Bobby's new gun and boxed his ears repeatedly right in front of us. Bobby cried, his fat body shaking, his little hands raised up against his uncle but not daring to touch him. He cried but he never told them it was my idea. As I followed her tiny figure back home, I definitely had new respect for my Chinese mother. When put into action she was formidable and I made sure that everybody in the playground knew who controlled this force.

But as I grew up this force focused on me and I was convinced she was incapable of love, that she hated me. She would look at me and hopelessly shake her head because for her everything was set in a cement called fate. It was inevitable that I was a fuck-up because my father was a guailo, a foreigner, a man she didn't love. Not that she missed being in love with a man. I don't think love entered into her scheme of existence. The very word, love, would make her scowl as if a large annoying fly had suddenly entered the room.

What Ma responded to was duty. It was her duty to marry a soldier in order to come to America and send money back to China so the rest of her family could come over. Once she got here she never expected to enjoy it. She endured it. All she thought of was money. What worried me was that I was the result of her sense of duty also. Sometimes I would catch her staring at me or mumbling in Chinese. Was there something else dark and Asian in my blood that I didn't know about, some force swimming in the black depths of my gene pool waiting to raise its dorsal fin out of the water? Was she trying to convince herself that I was more than just the ticket that got her married and into America? I worried, as only a child can worry, without any hope of being able to correct anything, until I couldn't stand it anymore.

That's when she became the horrible Dr Ming. Things were her fault not mine. When I started screaming back as all American teenagers eventually do, my mother considered herself a failure and stopped speaking to me altogether. By then I had found my mother's silence preferable. I didn't care anymore. If she didn't like how I was growing up, that was her fault. After all, it was her idea that I had grown up totally American.

I wasn't the only one she was mean to. She was mean to my dad too, because he was unemployed. She never yelled at him, she just wouldn't talk to him or look at him. It wasn't his fault. None of the dads in our town were working. It was the fault of the dark castles that stood one after another along the banks of the river. They loomed into the sky like the dwelling places of giants who performed unspeakable acts until an evil spell turned off their lights and closed their doors forever. Through snow and rain they stood deserted behind their cyclone fences bringing unemployment to all the land. If they weren't kept behind fences, the evil inside them would come alive and swallow up the earth. They all had names: Bethlehem Steel, Union Carbide, Carborundum Corp., Oxidental Chemical, Hooker Chemical, and the three M's, Minnesota Mining and Manufacturing. They were responsible for the silence that gripped the dinner table throughout my childhood as the dinner of scrambled eggs fell onto my plate and my father's head dropped into his hands.

When Ma stopped taking me to the casino, my father had to stay home and baby-sit me. I watched him balefully as he fumbled with my primer. Both of us grew to hate Jane and Dick and their dog Spot. We busied ourselves making up stories about how they got run over and fell down holes, and I grew to like my poor Dad. It wasn't like the spurned passion I wasted on Ma, it was a friendlier feeling built up night after night. The kind of feeling two prisoners can have for each other after years of enduring the same cell.

I complained about Ma to my dad, who I thought would be on my side, but he always had an excuse for her like, "Your mother is unhappy, kitten."

"Why? I didn't do anything wrong. She just hates me, that's all."

"No honey, she loves you. It's her family she's disappointed in. You see, she worked really hard to bring her parents and five brothers to the United States all the way from China and then, when they got here they went to Monterey Park in Southern California where it was warm and there is a large community of Chinese."

"You mean they never saw her?" It seemed incomprehensible to me.

"No."

"Why don't they come visit?"

"Because she lives with me. I'm a foreigner. It embarrasses them. And also, it's cold and strange here."

"So, she'll never see them again?"

"No, I don't think so. You see, she wasted a lot of her life and she didn't even get a thank you for it. And that's why she's unhappy, not because of you."

Then I felt terrible for her. And remembering my promise to the man with the long black hair who smelled of trees, I tormented myself with guilt and my anger vanished.

There were times my anger vanished long enough to hear her moaning and in spite of my fear of the hungry river spirit, I entered the dark forbidden bedroom. My mother was alone, her long black hair tangled like thin snakes all over the pillow. She seemed to be in such pain she didn't even notice me and didn't answer when I whispered her name. The only thing I could think of was that the little embroidered dragon that jumped around inside her got hungry and decided to make a lunch out of her liver. What could I do? Reach down her throat and pull him out? Try and trick him with a piece of food? For months after that, I made sure that there was always a piece of food hidden somewhere in her room.

3

The Gift

❧

WHY I CAN'T find my car? I've walked from one end of the parking lot to the other. I'm beginning to suspect that parking lots have been installed by the government as a test to see if you still qualify to be part of the human race. Of course, drink enough alcohol and who the fuck would want to belong to the hairless race of humans. The problem is I haven't drunk that much yet. Stray shopping carts follow me. Timidly they dislodge from where they have been abandoned and roll towards me like orphans after a barren woman who has come to adopt a child. If I were to accept one, to grab hold of its handle, it would latch onto me with the strength of a handcuff. I would become a bag woman, my clothes would morph into a shapeless mass, and my mind would liquefy into a dark pool swimming with prehistoric fears and helpless emotions.

Ignoring the carts, I walk on like I know where I parked. What kind of car did I drive? I can't even remember the color. Jesus, what if I came by bus? What if I'm poor? What's my bank balance? I catch my reflection, stretched and amputated on bits of chrome, tinted windows and mirrored surfaces. Long legs, long black hair, attractive but a little over-dressed for ten in the morning, a sign of neurosis or intense boredom? I'm young, so what's with the old and bitter act? A genetic fuck-up, or the wrong body due to a misfired reincarnation?

This isn't good. How many times can I wander up and down the parking lot before people notice? Better dump the Mallowmars, rearrange my hair, pretend I just arrived. I put my bag on a car and realize it's mine.

Quick, inside. There, I feel safe again. I close my eyes and listen for Niagara. It's actually traffic but if I drink enough, I can pretend the Falls are still near.

Sometimes when the wind blew to the west, the noise of the great Falls was so faint I would wake up in the middle of the night, afraid that it had abandoned me. But I only had to start walking towards Niagara and the roar would come back. No longer the whispering friend that kept me company during the night, it became a giant rolling great rocks along the echoing sky. The sound would vibrate your blood until it hit your chest with the wet thrill of sheer power. Ma hated that noise. For her it was the equivalent of helicopters as they blackened the sky, but for me it was as if my heart were being pounded like a drum. Once you got close to the Falls there was no going back until you had seen the explosion of light and water that the world calls Niagara, thousands of tons of water hitting the ground every split second, crashing and splintering upon itself from the stoic cliffs above.

Standing on the platform with my arms outstretched and my palms towards the torrent, I could feel the energy of the Falls enter my body, till I thought I would rise up in the air like an eagle. But the minute you let yourself feel this way you have to step back. Everyone who lived near the Falls and saw them every day knew about this feeling. It was more than dizziness, or a delirious fascination with power; it was the feeling that you could join the angels if you wanted to. That you could reach into the mist and lift the veil of immortality for a second, but woe to the tourist who stepped forward.

If it weren't for the guardrails more than one of them would have jumped to their watery death, mistaking it for eternal light. Perhaps that was why the Falls was the number one spot for suicides, the favorite leap for life's inconsolable lovers, the final resting place for elderly couples who wanted simply to go out together, and the ultimate test for failures who, unable to control life, at least imagined they were mastering their own deaths. As a candle cannot help drawing moths, the Falls drew the depressed, the tired, the weak, and the mystics who thought there must be a better place beyond reality, beyond the veil of tears that rose out of Niagara.

From the beginning, I believed in the magic of the Falls. I believed that all the energy that entered through the palms of my hands was stored in my body to be there when I needed it. Like when I raced Bobby Earlanger in front of the whole class. For most of the race I was forced to stare at Bobby's back and his short little legs hitting the dirt like pistons in a steam engine. Just as I thought I couldn't pass him the wind shifted and I heard Niagara pounding in my ears. The power of the

Falls was beside me like a great cat leaping over the grass. Bobby wasn't beating me, he was struggling to get away from me, his legs scrambling like a frightened goat. I didn't sink my teeth and claws into little Bobby's back, but I beat him, right in front of everybody. That day was the end of my friendship with fat Bobby. Accepted by the playground as a hero, I took my place among my peers, only to feel guilty whenever I saw Bobby playing our old games by himself. When no one was looking I would visit him.

Later on in high school I tested this strange power again and again as I continued to beat every girl on my swimming team. The little fish was growing into a very competitive fish, whose ruthlessness was a quality that only my mother's genes could be responsible for. The minute I felt my competition ahead of me I was like a shark after a wounded fish. Every muscle in my body would scream towards it until the water could not part fast enough. That's when my brain would whisper to my blood the magic word, Niagara, and the Falls would sweep me along. As I passed my fellow swimmer the image of teeth gutting open the body and pouring blood into the water like the bloom of a hungry red rose would push me over the finish line. Like clockwork, the thrill of this gruesome daydream was enacted at swim meet every Friday and I never tired of it. It brought me medals in the shape of gold coins on a ribbon very much like the lucky earrings my mother wore, and I was proud of them.

Of course, when I offered these medals to my mother, she was horrified that I was turning into such a jock. Being athletic or even strong was unforgivable in the female form. She worried about small feet and delicate hands and how I didn't have either. At sixteen, I was twice her size, but she never said anything because she wanted me to be completely American, and all Americans were tall due to their abnormal intake of aggressive amounts of red meat. She was convinced that red meat was the key to Americanism, and dinner always consisted of at least a half pound of flesh per person in the form of a steak, chop, or burger. The only Chinese food I ever got was in a restaurant.

I stare out of the window of my car, while the noise around me turns back into traffic. Let's face it, I'm a twenty-four-year-old drunk. On second thought let's not face it. Stuffing the key in the ignition, I race the motor which is what happens when you forget to put your car in gear. The sound attracts a patrol car. I fumble with my seatbelt. Yes, nurse, I can put on my own straightjacket, thank you. I rehearse what I'll say to the nice policeman. "Is that a breatholator or a blow job you are referring to? No, officer, I won't get out of my car because I left my legs home. I only have one pair and today is the day I wash them. They are probably flopping around in the dryer right now."

The cop car goes off in another direction, lights flashing and siren blaring with self-importance. I pull a bottle of vodka from the glove compartment. Well, you see, officer, since my brother Kenny disappeared I've been drinking a little . . . it runs in the family, but I'm not going to get into that. Well, cheers. Here's to it.

Shit.

Here I am trying to have a good time, and staring me in the face is a billboard with Niagara Falls on it. My beautiful lovely Niagara finally silenced, frozen in a beer commercial. Damn it, I hate drunks who get all weepy.

Tears bring the memory of my brother, Kenny, back. Shit again. The whole reason for drinking is to forget he is gone. You see, I thought he was a gift, but he was just a loan. Niagara couldn't bear to be without him anymore than I could, and so he was taken back.

The gift came in the middle of the night after a thunderstorm had just pounded across the land like an army of advancing horsemen. My dad woke me up, saying he had a surprise for me. As we walked to the car the wind smelled of rain and lightning crackled along the river, lighting up the night sky. My dad was the only one who seemed to care how lonely I was, so I thought he had bought me a pet of some sort. I figured it had to be a cat or hopefully a dog, but when I looked in the car there was a pale child staring back at me. His skin was so white it looked fragile, as if his veins were shadows of cracks in the thinnest translucent china. His hair was curly black and long like a girl's. And he had thick black lashes surrounding green eyes that were so bright they gleamed like chips of cut glass as they stared out of the depths of the car.

"He's your new brother." My father leaned over me and I smelled the pickled odor of booze. "His name is Kenny. I found him under the Falls."

I had no reason not to believe Dad because his clothes and hair were soaking wet, and he had been gone two weeks, exactly how long I thought it must take to make such a journey to the secret caves under the Falls.

"Of course, he'll look more like your brother once we give him a crew cut and get some food in him." Dad was so happy he was practically dancing around the car. God only knows how many bars he had stopped in along the way. Kenny watched his new dad from under frowning black brows and refused to get out of the car. Right away, I could tell he hated the idea of a haircut. He didn't seemed pleased with his new father either.

The strange boy glowered at us as Dad pulled him out of the car. "I want monkey back."

"You're too old to have a stuffed animal," Dad snapped back.

Without a word the boy turned and started down the driveway. Dad had to run after him and drag him back like a prisoner.

"I have stuffed animals. You can have one of mine," I told him.

"No. I want monkey back."

"We can buy him another monkey, can't we," I pleaded.

"No, we can't." My father's voice was turning ugly.

"Yes, we can." Ma ended the conversation. The strange boy stopped struggling and stood on his own. He was a skinny little child, and I thought he was beautiful. I didn't care if he was a hungry river spirit in disguise or if he had been stolen from the giant in the Falls, I wanted him to stay with us forever.

I wasn't the only one who fell in love with the strange child in the back of Dad's car that night. Watching Ma's long red nails slide through Kenny's hair again and again I suspected she was trying to take possession of him. How I wanted those sharp nails to tear passionately at my skin. She pulled his head to her chest and my insides smoldered in green flames. He was my gift, for me and me alone, and I didn't want anyone else touching him, especially her.

In spite of all my efforts to keep them apart, there did seem to be this strange connection between Kenny and Ma, which I was left out of. I hated to admit it, but both Ma and Kenny had similarities, each mysterious, each manipulative, and each with a dark past. Kenny never spoke of his real mother. She and my father had been high school sweethearts forced into an early marriage after he knocked her up. While Dad was in the army, his pretty wife left him and overdosed in the Haight Ashbury. Dad found out while he was in Vietnam, and that was when he met my mom.

Ma never mentioned her past either. No one did. It was as if she didn't have any. Yet she had a thick Chinese accent and a face that could never be mistaken for a native of western New York. As a family we ignored this, pretending she was no different than any of the other school moms. But Ma was painfully shy with the neighbors and insisted that Dad do all the PTA stuff.

When Kenny first arrived with the manners of a stray cat, it was Ma who tamed him. She seemed to welcome this child like the dark side of her own life, and in spite of herself she loved him. She loved him in a way she never loved me. I couldn't understand it. She was like a hermit who in order to escape the dangers of love, denies herself any emotional contact. One day she pets a cat that meows at her window. It's a skinny cat and it's starving to death, so she begins to feed it. When it rains she lets it inside and it keeps her company. It purrs in gratitude so she lets it sleep in bed with her. Every day she talks to it, feeds it, and sleeps with it, and at the end of a year when it doesn't come home her life has a big ugly hole in it. The one thing that she loved is missing and she has escaped nothing. She should never have touched his dark hair like that.

If you lived in our house, there were two things you had to accept about my mother. First, the only thing she loved was money. She had sticky fingers; money did not pass through her hands, it stayed there. If I asked her to save the allowance my dad gave me, whether it was a quarter or ten dollars, I never saw it again. Secondly, the only person Ma wasted any emotion on (for her, emotion was a waste) was my stepbrother Kenny. My problem was, I didn't accept the latter of these things. With envy I watched my brother tip the scales of Ma's heart. He was almost more important to her than money, and it made my blood boil.

To my dad's disappointment, Kenny and he never bonded the way a father and son are supposed to. Instead I remained my father's favorite tomboy as Kenny crouched in the seat of favor under Ma's powerful dragon's wing.

Even after it was explained to me that Kenny was Dad's son from a previous marriage, and that Dad was wet that night because he had to change a tire in a thunderstorm twenty minutes away; even after they gave Kenny a crew cut, and he looked like a shaved rabbit, I still chose to believe that he was my gift stolen from the caves under the Falls. Let's face it, the whole fucked-up family was in love with Kenny. That's why my parents drank, and that's why I started drinking. Because he's gone.

4

East of the sun

HEARING A TAPPING on my window, I look out and see
this kid, the box boy from the supermarket, staring at
me. His eyes are haunted as he carefully puts two fingers
to his lips and lowers them. Rolling down the window,
I can't imagine what he wants. "What?" is all I can
think to say.

"Buy some weed?"

"What?"

Confidently he saunters over to the car and leans in
the window. "Marhiwana, lady. It's better for you than
that stuff."

I put the top on the half empty bottle of vodka beside
me. "You're selling dope? In broad daylight like this?"

The child grins, "I sell to a lot of housewives here.
You were sitting in your car, I thought you were a new
customer."

"Here, do you need money? All I have are twenties."
I fumble for my purse.

"They're already rolled." He tosses a baggy through the window.

"No, I don't want any."

"Yes, you do. You need it." Before I can give the bag back to him, he is gone.

Tossing the pot out the window as if it were radioactive, I pull out of the parking lot a little too fast and almost go through a red light. Even the box boys here are too hip for me. To keep my sanity, I have started driving more and more, like to Santa Barbara and back to get the same chicken I could get at Vons only four blocks away. Traffic, of course, is hell. I pack food to eat and a glass jar to piss in. But most of the time being on the freeway is like having a transfusion. As long as I'm moving, moving, anonymity, animosity, cruising up to sixty-five, seventy, eighty-five. OOPS, I almost rear-end a baby on board. Time to drive to the oil derricks and calm down. The little herd of derricks on the Stockard Pass as you approach the Los Angeles airport comes into view, iron animals placidly giving the planet a nice slow methodical hand job, big old bony things going up and down. I am happy now. I drive fast, but not fast enough. The memories catch up to me, clogging my sense of smell, my hearing, and finally I don't see what's in front of me. I see trees that can gallop and clouds that are castles.

After Kenny arrived, I forgot about being exiled from the casino because with Kenny everything was turned into fantasy. A group of trees would no longer be bark and leaves, it would be an emissary from the Court of King Arthur that had ridden across the valley and now stood at full salute waiting for us to approach. The grove of ancient oaks formed the cathedral where we knelt for hours to pledge allegiance to our king before entering the battle where we would die for him. One burnt-out old tree, which was big enough for us to hide in, was the prison where Kenny was tied up naked and tortured by the evil queen of everything mucky and slimy. I would have to wait behind the rocks listening to his painful moaning until he gave the signal to be rescued. Sometimes this would go on too long or sound too real, and I would jump the gun, which was terrible because then we would have to start all over. Kenny was a stickler for things being just right, except for when it came to dying. Then, even when the story called for a princess to die, Kenny had to be the one who did the dying. We traded clothing with each other all the way down to the underwear, so he could be the girl. I could argue till I was blue in the face, but Kenny insisted. He had a gift for persuasion, not that I needed much persuasion. I didn't like to see him hurt or not getting what he wanted.

Our favorite game was death. Kenny was in love with dying. He was constantly either lying for hours in the dirt and leaves, or dramatically poised on a cliff while gasping his last breath, or laid out on a makeshift bed of flowers with hands across his chest. And I was always running down hills with the rescuing army, climbing up mountains with the antidote, or in constant mourning at his grave because, as usual, I was too late. The only time I got to die was when we re-enacted the Indian myth of Niagara, then I would be the Indian princess, and he would be my Indian lover dying while trying to save me.

Everyone in Niagara Falls knew the myth. It was an

old Indian tale that we firmly believed in. Every year the Indian tribe that used to live near the Falls sacrificed the most beautiful virgin of the tribe to the god of the Falls. They would put her in a canoe filled with flowers and send her over the edge to her death. One year it happened to be the chief's daughter that was chosen. As he watched her drift towards the edge, the old chief couldn't stand it. He jumped in his canoe and tried to save her, but by the time he reached her, the hunger of the Falls was too great and they both fell to their deaths. The legend says that the mists over Niagara are her tears, and the roar of Niagara is his cry of anguish.

To this day the small town of Niagara still celebrates the Falls with this myth. Our school chooses an Indian princess from the senior class, who they put in a canoe filled with flowers, and pull down Main Street to the beat of the school tomahawk drum corps. At the Falls the quarterback of the football team lifts her out, and the canoe of flowers is set in the water and allowed to drift over the edge. Standing on the sidewalk to see this yearly parade, Kenny and I were always depressed that they didn't leave the princess in her boat. What kind of a sacrifice was a boat without a victim? Was it any wonder we all had such bad luck, when every year we cheated the Falls with this mockery?

Our only recourse was to make a childhood pact to do it right when our turn came. If I was chosen to be the Indian princess in my senior year, I would stay in my boat all the way to the end, and Kenny would go after me, but, of course, it would be too late. We would die together, and Ma and Dad would be grief-stricken, and very sorry they didn't treat us better. Luckily this absurd plan was not going to take effect any time soon because neither of us was in high school yet. We were in grade school, a dismal place where boys hung out with boys and the girls banded together, except for me. I was Asian, and I thought the only other Asian girls in my class, two very dorky Japanese sisters, were beneath me. So I hung out alone, since fat Bobby didn't really count. But everything changed when Kenny came into my life. I didn't care about anyone else. The problem was that Kenny turned out to be very social and after the first summer of having him all to myself I had to share him. The only time I felt alive was when Kenny let me tag along with him, but as he became more popular, this happened less and less.

The final slap in the face came when Kenny announced that I was no longer welcome in the tree house that had been our secret place for so long. It all happened one lazy summer day while we were riding our bikes back from swimming. Because I was such a good swimmer, I was the only girl they let come along. Fiercely proud of this arrangement, I was devastated when Kenny and his friends turned off into the woods and I was told not to follow them.

"Why? I know where you're going. Why can't I come?"

"Because it's no girls allowed," Kenny's eyes glittered bright green while the other boys looked at the ground. It made it worse that Fat Bobby was one of them. I had dropped him and now it was his turn to dump me.

"But it's my tree house too."

"No, it's the club house now."

"That's not fair." I wasn't going to cry. That was the most important thing, not to cry in front of them.

"Yes, it is," Kenny was adamant.

"Let her come with us," Bobby said, but he said it so low, I knew it was hopeless.

"No, if she comes, then it will not be a club house." Kenny pushed my bike over, making me get off. "Don't follow us. And don't cry. Go home, Mei Li." I hated him for using my Chinese name in front of the others. The next day the same thing happened, so I stopped swimming with them altogether.

Those were the black years, when I was excluded from the inner goings on of the club house. Exiled again, this time was worse because it was the trees and the sky, not just the inside of a casino that I was thrown out of. But I knew not to beg. Begging got you nowhere. It didn't work with Ma, and I knew it would never work with Kenny. Instead, I didn't talk to Kenny for a month. I was as mute as sleeping beauty. In my wretched tomb of silence where I stumbled around like the walking dead, my fevered brain hatched plan after plan, plans as bizarre as marrying Kenny so he could never get rid of me again. We would live far away and he would be a prisoner of my love.

Soon, like sleeping beauty I was brought back to life. Although Kenny and his new friends spent a lot of time in their precious club house, he wasn't about to give up his love affair with dying. So, when he needed me in his next adventure – project barrel – I didn't stay mad at him. Gratefully I returned from exile, but it wasn't the same. The rocks were no longer an ambush waiting to happen, the clouds ceased to be the unfurling banners of the approaching battle we were to die in, and the forest was only a forest. Now I had to share my brother with his new friends, a pack of crude boys from school.

And swallowing my pride, I pretended not to notice, when they marched off to the private club house.

Our Indian princess myth was forgotten in the wake of project barrel; Kenny's new plan was to be famous as the youngest daredevil to go over the Falls in a specially constructed barrel. This obsession of Kenny's supplanted all our old games. It took over everything. The only thing that mattered was the barrel, and I went from the dramatic rescuer of all to a mere assistant in project barrel.

5

Project barrel

THIS TIME I DO have a small accident with the curb. Get it together, will you. Maybe I need more lipstick? Maybe I should wind this sucker up to one hundred and then sit on the gearshift. I overtake a Porsche. Is it Richard Gere thinking of taking me to the Marriott for a quickie? No, just another neurotic-looking woman with red eyes and thin white lips, as if all her lipstick had migrated to her eyeballs. I raise my bottle of vodka in a toast, and she gives me the finger. People are so pleasant if you give them a chance. Now, where was I?

Project barrel, it was an absurd idea. I didn't believe that Kenny would go over the Falls any more than I believed he was going to burn himself at the stake. Yet after he announced that he was Kenny D'Arc, I spent weeks putting him on trial, days gathering branches and twigs to pile around the stake, and nights inventing stories that would explain the scorch marks on my night gown which he had decided to wear on his death. Thankfully, the night that Kenny D'Arc was supposed to fry for all the unjust things I had to accuse him of, it rained. Similarly, I supposed that the day we would launch the barrel with my brother neatly tucked up inside it, Niagara would simply not be working. So, completely free of any guilt, I threw myself into the project.

The only other kid we let in on our secret project was Bobby, who was no longer fat. He had grown from shorter than me to twice my size in one year, but as far as I was concerned, he would always be fat Bobby. I thought it was unfair that he could grow so out of reach. The idea of beating him in a race was definitely out of the question now. No one could beat him. It was another cruel joke Mother Nature had played on us. I particularly didn't like it that Bobby was becoming Kenny's best friend.

It happened at junior football practice, something Dad insisted on in order to build up his son's frail body. Dad was constantly pushing Kenny into any kind of macho activity he could. He even dragged his underage son to the bars that he frequented. But Kenny put a stop to that by ordering milk.

However, it wasn't that easy to get out of football. The sight of Kenny rattling around in his football uniform like a broom in a closet was truly pathetic. His neck was so small and his helmet so big, it looked like his head was going to wobble off it. And his shoulder pads looked like a new pair of ill fitting wings. Both Ma and I refused to watch any of the games. But we needn't have worried. Kenny threw himself into the sport with such determination and so little ability that the coach eventually sent him home saying that he feared for his life. Dad sent him right back saying, Come hell or high water his son was going to play football. He even insisted that Kenny play center, which made me wonder if Dad might be trying to kill Kenny.

Coach Stedman grew to hate Kenny, who turned out to be a troublemaker and a dirty player, but for some baffling reason, the other boys seemed afraid of him, or at least hesitant to turn against him even when he called them names. Bobby protected him; it was as if a wolverine had befriended an elephant much to the consternation of the rest of the jungle. They were a perfect union of opposites; Bobby, the big strong shy boy, and Kenny, the weak cunning bully. I guess it was all the beatings Bobby's uncle gave him that made him a good fighter because he wasn't really aggressive. But as Kenny developed his knack for getting into fights, Bobby unwittingly took over my job of coming to his rescue.

I felt better when I realized that protection was the reason Kenny became friends with Bobby, but I still didn't want Bobby in on our adventures. Kenny insisted, "He's very strong and we need the help. Also, he knows how to make things out of wood. We'll put him in charge of barrel construction." I didn't want to argue. From then on, he and Kenny were always together concocting and arguing over the perfect barrel to go over the Falls in.

Kenny was the master planner and pilot.

Bobby was head of barrel construction.

I was in charge of gathering information and facts.

A – 200,000 cubic feet of water per second go over the
    Falls.
    12,000,000 cubic feet of water per minute.
    1 cubic foot = eight gallons.

It's interesting because I have looked at the Falls for exactly a minute and I know what 12,000,000 cubic feet looks like.

B – The Falls are 1,075 feet high.
C – The Falls have frozen twice: 1840, 1930.
*   The wind comes from the left, where it first rides across the Great Plains, then screams across the Great Lakes to pile ice in the river. Like the hordes of Ghengis Khan, nothing can stop it.*
D – Lake Erie is 55 miles wide, 250 miles long and empties into the river Niagara. The north shores of Lake Erie are beautiful beaches where all the rich kids in my class have summer cabins.
E – Niagara is the only river that runs north.

Bobby goes with me to the library and museum for photos and facts about jumpers and their different methods. I told him, I don't need his help. I am the collector of information. It's my job, but he comes along anyway.

A – The fist person to go over the Falls in 1901 was a woman, Winnie Edson Taylor. She was a prim school marm from Michigan. She was sixty years old, wore a long dress, and went over in a barrel. Her manager left with the money before she was found. She only had a cut on the jaw. She used a tall barrel with an anchor on the bottom. Fifteen more people try to go over the Falls; all are men, and only eight or nine live.

Actually, Bobby is being nice. He comes to help me all the time now and without him, I would be pretty bored. I make him tell me what they do in the club house that's so secret. He gets all embarrassed but I am relentless. He says Kenny gets them cigarettes and old *Playboy* magazines, and they put up pictures of naked girls. It sounds pretty dumb, and I'm glad I'm not there.

B – George Stalakis attached his wrists to the top of a barrel, an anvil to his ankles, and an anchor to the bottom of the barrel. Result – his legs and the anvil went through the bottom of the barrel while his arms and head stayed inside.

Bobby says the weirdest things. He says he'd do anything I want him to do. When I ask him why, he says he doesn't know, he just would. Then he looks at me with his brown eyes. Bobby has dog eyes; they can stare at you for the longest time without blinking. There's nothing I want you to do, I tell him, and he sighs like I just put a collar on him and tied him to the fence.

C – William Redhill went through the rapids. (So I wrote his name down but that's not going over the Falls.)

Bobby tried to kiss me. He did kiss me. I don't know how it happened. We were in the library trying to be quiet, when he leaned over to whisper something in my ear, but he missed my ear and suddenly his lips were on my mouth. I couldn't make any noise. It was so quick, I didn't stop him, I was so confused, I forgot to stop him and he got to stick his tongue in my mouth. Bobby also pulled away first, and when he did, he had a big grin on his face. I was mortified.

D – William Redhill Jr. in an attempt to outdo his father went over the Falls in a barrel with a steel base. He was held

under the Falls for days. He suffocated or maybe he starved
to death, I don't know which would come first.

Bobby is becoming a nuisance. He just wants to fool
around. I had to put my foot down. I told him he has to
stop because this is serious business, and that was final,
or I would tell Kenny. When I did tell Kenny, his green
eyes went black with anger, not at Bobby, but at me. He
told me hideous stories of babies getting caught in their
mother's stomachs and having to eat their way out, of
venereal diseases that make your blood explode, your
brain rot, and all your teeth fall out. And he said if Ma
or Dad found out I would be sent away to a correctional
facility where they sew your mouth and your vagina up
and make you do laundry till you drop dead.

Now, of course, we have space shuttle barrels and jumping is called stunting. Kenny looks down on this method.
There is a large fee for pulling them out, much more than
we can afford. So, it's a good thing Kenny plans on
doing it the old way and Bobby and I are behind him.

While I collected stories and information about
people's daredevil attempts to conquer the Falls in
barrels, boxes, and special capsules, Kenny prepared
himself mentally and physically for the big jump. He
tried everything: diets, work-outs, but the worst were
the endurance tests. There were three kinds: pain, coldness, and staying in a cramped position for a long time.
For pain he wanted me to burn him with a candle or
cut him with scissors, but these tests never went very far
because I would freak out. Tying him up in weird positions thankfully only lasted ten or fifteen minutes
because it was so boring.

As for the cold endurance testing, it was outlawed.

When Ma caught him taking one of his cold showers with the hose in the back yard in mid-winter, she forbade any more tests, plans, or even mention of daredevil attempts. But she was too late. The Falls became such an obsession with Kenny, the testing went on in secret until he got sick, sick enough to be rushed to the hospital. In the cold white waiting room of the hospital, I saw Ma cry. She collapsed like a gray ghost into sobs so painful that Dad had to hold her in his arms to keep her from breaking apart. Watching her, I realized this was the real reason Ma hated the Falls. She was afraid they could somehow lure Kenny to his death and she was powerless to protect him. The house of the evil spirit is what she called the Falls, but she didn't fool me. I told her if she watched more TV like other parents instead of gambling all night she would know there were no evil spirits.

Secretly, however, I thought she might be right. Night and day the water spilled down, as if a main artery in the neck of the planet had been fatally cut. I could never explain the fear and fascination I felt until I saw *The Wizard of Oz*. When the witch turned the giant hour glass over, and Dorothy knew that the sands of life were running through that opening, I understood that Niagara was the hour glass of the world, and when the water ran out, all would be gone. Life would come to an end, and black emptiness would fall upon the land. It made me want to stop the water from rushing over the edge, but one look at mighty Niagara and I knew that was impossible. No one could stop it, no one could slow it down, you couldn't even focus on any-thing once it started falling over the edge.

6

The ballbreaker

Zipping on to the Santa Monica freeway, I manage to keep it at eighty miles an hour by negotiating some spectacular lane changes, slowing only slightly to enter the Harbor freeway, which is always pure pleasure due to the slightly sci-fi look of downtown Los Angeles. At the Hollywood freeway traffic starts seizing up, turning my pleasant buzz slightly grumpy. Escaping the Hollywood freeway, I turn onto the San Bernardino freeway right into rush hour traffic. Nothing, I repeat, nothing is worse than rush hour traffic. The San Bernardino freeway is always a flat piece of straight gridlock hell, and I always forget to get off until it's too late. People kill when trapped in the frustration of gridlock. I am no different and since no other victim is around I strap on my sharpest teeth and start in on my own arm. Next is my ego, where is my ego – I put it somewhere in here . . . here we go. My name is Molly Carson and I'm a bitch. Believe me, my husband is lucky I drink. I have a perfectly good marriage to a man who loves me and all I can do is break the poor guy's balls. I can't help it. It's in my genes. It's my mother's fault. Looking back on the cartoon disaster that is my family, my mother was the embodiment of the evil Dr Ming.

It was Ma who was to blame for Dad's failure. She was the one who made him sleep in the back room like a ghost shut in the closet. But since Dr Ming was masquerading as the good Chinese mother, Dad's unemployment was blamed on alcohol. In our family, we blamed almost everything on alcohol. Of course, my dad drank. Everyone from the fifties drank. Everybody in this neck of the woods drank, especially during the bleak Arctic months of winter. I drank like a fish all through high school. My dad drank because he was a man and men drink together in bars, especially when they're out of work.

At first my mother, who had lost everything including her country, could not understand the depression that made him silent, that made him drink, and that made him lose interest in her. Unhappy and insecure in her new country, she worried that she wasn't pleasing him. She couldn't believe he was sitting in a bar instead of lying in the arms of another woman. All of this paranoia was aggravated by a difficult pregnancy. From inside her belly I could hear the voice of my father, "May, please stop it. I'm never going to leave you. Just try, try and believe me." It echoed through the house before he stomped out the door, leaving her alone. So, she drank to keep him company. It was enough that she was married and living in America, but when I was born, it wasn't enough. Believing that her charms were no longer appealing she fell back on the only other talent she brought with her from her days as a prostitute. She began gambling professionally with me tied to her back. It's ironic that the most contented years of my life were terrible years for my mother, and I believe that it was during this time that Dr Ming emerged.

Soon Dad was coming home drunk night after night to find my mother gone, and somewhere along the line my father changed from a man who drinks to a drunk. I didn't notice the change in Dad right away because drunk or sober he always had a smile for me. But I was very aware of the new look on Ma's face, as he sat down to dinner. The way Dr Ming served his food was tainted with just enough disgust to make me uncomfortable for him. But he said nothing since he was still unemployed and she was bringing home the money. He was forced to accept everything she did.

My mother's grip on my father's balls tightened as the reigns slipped from my father's fingers. The weaker he became the more confident she grew. For Dr Ming, security was controlling the purse strings, and every night she returned from the casino a little more in control. What puzzled me was that when Dr Ming came back from the casino with her purse stuffed full of money, her attitude didn't change. All the money she won didn't make her happy. She never laughed. The punishing silence still covered our food like fine dust.

If it hadn't been for Ming's shrewdness with money, not to mention the fact that she had a calculator for a heart and uncanny luck at the casino, we would have been poor and my dad might have been an average father. But little by little we stopped being poor. Ma bought a new house and to my embarrassment, Dad was made to sleep in the little bedroom in the back. Dr

Ming said it was because she had to sleep all day and he was an early riser. But that wasn't the real reason. The real reason was that my father was giving up his position as head of the house. Without a whimper, Dad went to his room with his tail between his legs. From then on, he no longer looked for work. He was my baby-sitter, while the evil Dr Ming went gambling without me.

I was so miserable at being left at home that Dad was alarmed. Like someone who has one lonely dog he keeps in the back yard and, instead of letting it in the house, he buys another dog to keep it company, Dad brought home a stray to console me. It turned out to be the worst thing he could have done. If there had been no Kenny I think Dad would have been quite happy to quietly drink himself to death in the back room. But Kenny never let him rest, not for a minute, and it was because of Kenny that Dad refused to disappear into the back room and insisted on sitting at the dining room table night after night, drunkenly going on and on about what? None of us could ever understand it. He felt compelled to push Kenny to be the macho son he wanted, and at every step Kenny rebelled in the most maniacal ways. It was hard for me to watch because Dad was no match for Kenny and I felt sorry for him.

When Kenny didn't go to the college Dad was so proud he had gotten into, something in him snapped. Night after night he hounded Kenny for being a failure. He picked on him relentlessly, saying derogatory things about him as if he wasn't sitting at the same dinner table. It was always the same theme – failure – my dad's intense fear of failure. Not only had he lost his own job but his son was a tour guide on a sightseeing boat. "What kind of a future was that? Telling a lot of stupid people that the greatest waterfall in the world was right in front of their noses. What was he going to do for the rest of his life?" But none of us thought he cared about Kenny's future. As his drinking increased we were convinced that he cared about very little.

I hated listening to Dad blaming Kenny for his own failure. Dad lost his job at the plant before Kenny ever arrived, and he could never seem to get another one. Dad said it was because of Vietnam, and maybe it was, but I didn't understand. He was tall and strong. The only weak part about him were his eyes. They were small blue eyes that looked frightened like the eyes of a little animal in the wrong body.

These tirades always ended up with Dad staring across the table at Ma and me, unable to understand why the women in his family didn't back him. Our scowling silence dragged all his arguments into murky waters where he felt more like the culprit than his too-smart-for-his-own-good son. The distant sound of Niagara filled his head, reminding him of his high blood pressure.

In the hallway Ma would run after Kenny, pulling off his hat and gloves, while the wind screamed outside and the red sun sank below the banks of dirty snow. First she would grip his face to make him look at her. He stared back at her with the eyes of a stray cat. Remembering that look from when she first met him, she must have known it was hopeless. She told him his father still loved him and that she loved him too even though she was not his mom. Her fingers would slide through his dark hair and he would let her unbutton the hunting jacket Dad gave him. By the time he followed Ma back to the table, Dad would have vanished into his room like the ghost he was.

All the time she yelled at me, Ma never raised her voice to Kenny. I thought that was sexist, and when I pointed out to her how unfair she was being, she replied in a matter of fact voice, "A man's ego is fragile like a snake's egg. If you break it, evil will be free to slither over the land, poisoning whatever heart it bites into." How can you reason with someone who thinks like that?

Ma didn't use reason much. She never went to school. She said because her parents were poor, she was sent to work – the kind of work where you never saw your parents again. I figured that she was a prostitute and maybe a spy, a criminal and a hero, which fit in with how I felt about her. With a background like that it was no wonder that she relied mostly on instinct, and Ma's instincts were scary. She had a way of going quiet before she did anything and I could tell she was listening to the currents in the air that carried voices. She could also feel the secret tremors that ran along the ground bearing the tiny warnings of aftermaths to come. There was definitely something primal about her – almost reptilian. She lay hidden in her room for most of the day the way a lizard waits under its rock for the sun to go away. When we were young, Kenny and I called her room the opium den. It was always dark and smelled of incense, and we had to tiptoe by the door because it was a secret place where the dragon slept and everyone was afraid of waking it up.

By high school, Kenny had the same nocturnal habits as Ma, while I fell asleep all scrunched up in my chair, trying to stay up, watching the late late show, waiting for them to come home. Try as I might I couldn't keep my eyes open past eleven. It was infuriating. Nor could I sleep late. Even on Saturdays and Sundays, I was the stupid early bird, getting up for breakfast with Dad who, no matter how much he drank, was up at the crack of dawn making coffee, pancakes, left-over ham or steak sandwiches for our school lunch.

Actually, I liked the quiet morning time with my dad, when the rest of the house was sleeping. He never talked much when he was sober but in that silence I could feel him, keeping me company. He loved to tinker when he wasn't drunk, to have a job to do. If the table was wobbling he would fix it, or the roof, or the drain. If it had snowed the night before he would be outside shoveling the walk. And I would help him, just because I liked being near him.

Ma wasn't like that. Housework could put her in a very bad mood. She was the schemer, the plotter, and the diplomat, all behind a mask-like face that told you nothing. I was sick of the fuss she made over Kenny. I could have told her she didn't have to protect him. He was more than able to look after himself. But she never listened to me anyway.

Kenny retaliated against my father with his most lethal weapon, his tongue. At first he just did little things to get back at Dad, like telling me lies behind his back.

"You know Dad's finger that was cut off at the plant, and that's the reason he can't work any more?"

"Yes. What about it?"

"Well, he cut it off himself in a bar because someone dared him to do it. He's a drunken fool, and he'll do anything to forget that he's a coward."

"What are you talking about, Kenny? He got it cut off trying to save – "

"Bullshit." Kenny cut me off, his eyes the color of Seven Up bottles. "And do you know why he's always getting in fights and doing crazy things? To prove he is a man, because in the Army he wasn't in combat. He was one of those guys who interrogate prisoners. He tortured people."

"That's not true, Kenny."

"He put electrodes on prisoners' nuts – "

"How do you know this?"

"And if they were female, he did it to their breasts."

"Who told you this?"

"The bartenders in the local bars around here. He's famous all over town for being an asshole. He gets drunk and blabs his whole life story to the bartenders and when they're so bored they can't listen anymore, he does crazy things like cutting off his finger to get their attention."

It was like letting him drop poison into my ear. Even though I tried not to believe Kenny my feelings for my father changed. I didn't fear or hate him. I was embarrassed for him in a way that hurt my heart but also paralyzed me against doing anything about it. Too uncomfortable around him to enjoy our ritual of morning breakfast together, I began sleeping late, or pretending to sleep late. When he said he missed me, I didn't answer him, but I still ate the cold pancakes he left out for me.

Finally Kenny just flat out called our father a coward to his face. Not in a loud voice – he wasn't angry. He had a smirk as he said, "The whole town knows you're a coward. I'm going to prove to everyone that I'm not like you. No one is going to call me a coward because I'm going over the Falls." I stopped breathing as he said the words, "going over the Falls." It was our old childhood fantasy, but nobody ever expected him to really do it. It had to be a joke. I listened for the sound of Niagara but the howling wind drowned everything out. That night one of the worst blizzards in a decade arrived and stayed a week. As billions of white flakes swirled madly around our house, Kenny started building a barrel in the basement, the kind daredevils use to go over the Falls in. The idea was ridiculous, but Kenny was so relentless, we all became frightened of the barrel's menacing presence. The days went by, snow-locking everyone in the house behind six- and seven-foot drifts. Dad would spend the whole day trying to clear the drive, but even then you couldn't go any-where. Finally he gave up and joined us as we listened to the tapping of Kenny's hammer echoing up the base-ment steps.

When the snow stopped falling and the sun re-entered the world, we were not the same family. The storm had given birth to a new member in our family – the barrel. It was like an alien in the house, suffocating us by taking up the silent space inside everyone's head. The more shape it took on, the more power it pos-sessed. Sometimes Kenny would tear it down and start all over. Then it would get even stronger. When the house was quiet I could hear it waiting for Kenny's hands to come back and feed it. It waited like the dark castles locked away behind their cyclone fences, ban-ishing any trace of laughter from the house by making us all feel vaguely depressed all the time. Every night after he finished working, Kenny locked the basement door behind him.

In the coming months, whenever Kenny wanted to get back at Dad, all he had to do was go downstairs and work on his barrel. The more Dad called him a failure, the farther into the night Kenny worked, and the later Dad stayed up and drank. He drank till his hands shook in the morning, and he couldn't eat anything for breakfast. Grimly he shoveled the walk every morning of every bit of melting snow or crust of left-over ice, and sometimes he shoveled it when there wasn't any snow.

7

The sacrifice

DRIVING UP TO my garage door two and a half hours later, I stop and stare at it. Open up, you fucking moron, you think I'm sitting here for my health? So I forgot the clicker, so what. You'd think just once it would open without the clicker. That's a reasonable request, isn't it? I mean, I drive into this garage enough times, you'd think it'd know what to do. We just did this yesterday for the seventeen millionth time. Remember? You open up, and I go in, so how about some fucking cooperation? Huh? I'm so sloshed I can't do anything but stare at the door. After about five minutes of staring, I get out of the car, and I'm trapped on a useless piece of greenery called a front lawn. I lie down on the grass with my face to the sun. When I close my eyes I see blood. I gotta smile, this is so illegal. If anyone found me like this their first question would be, "What's wrong?" And then, "Mr Earlanger, your wife is lying on the front lawn." "Oh my God, does she have her clothes on? Is she bleeding?"

The sun is quiet and warm on my face. Hummm, I know this feeling. Sleep is around here somewhere. There it is, to the left, the silver river. I slip into it, and I've escaped without moving a muscle. My skull is a vacation . . . except for that tapping sound. I need to sleep but I can't. The tapping sound . . . I can't ignore it. Soon it fills my head. It is the only thing I can hear. It scares me because it's not supposed to be here. It's coming all the way from the basement of our house in Niagara. It's the sound of Kenny's hammer building the barrel. It's not very loud, but it is loud enough to shatter all the fragile glass thoughts that I keep on the shelf in my head. It shatters any hope I have of sleep. To get rid of the tapping, I usually drink but today, it's not working. The tapping continues later and later into the night.

Kenny was serious enough to convince Bobby to come over and help him in his dark endeavor. This time it wasn't a childhood fantasy. It was two adults fully capable of carrying out their mad scheme. I couldn't understand it and I wanted no part of it. Together they worked furiously on testing barrels that would survive the ultimate test. The effort and time both boys were putting into barrel construction was frightening.

Bobby's eyes followed me around hopelessly whenever he came over. I didn't know if he was coming over to help Kenny or be near me. I was relieved when it became evident that he was hanging around our house because of me and not because he believed in the barrel. Every time he came over he would bring me something: a smooth black rock from the river, pussy willows in the spring or acorns in the fall, a sea shell from an ocean a million miles away. Other times he would bring me a twisted piece of metal from the deserted factories up river, or a pretty colored piece of glass he found imbedded in the earth. I used to tell him he should be a sculptor and glue all these things together, but he never did. Kenny kept him too busy.

Little fat Bobby had turned into one of those big football guys, nice enough, but kind of dumb, or at least I thought so. It was hard not to think otherwise the way Kenny talked behind his back about his thick neck and slow wit. Still, I liked him. It was Kenny who convinced me that Bobby was dumb instead of shy. Of course, Kenny was so facile with his tongue, he could convince me that a rabbit was a predatory monster while the poor misunderstood alligator deserved all my love, attention, and undying devotion. In the jungles of my imagination this could happen. The problem was I ventured into the forest of reality thinking like this and when giant discrepancies arose I did my best to change the forest into the jungle rather than disbelieve my brother. After all if I didn't believe him, I would never have known how the people felt when they gathered wood to burn poor Joan of Arc. So, Kenny's word was gospel and I remained a devout believer in order not to lose the child of my past.

I think one of Kenny's problems was he was bored, and it made him sarcastic. His mouth was always getting him into trouble. If it wasn't for Bobby being Kenny's bodyguard all through our childhood, he would have been wasted long ago. Bobby saved his ass twice, once when he called the opposing team a bunch of cock-sucking faggots, and another time when he attacked Mark Mullen, who has seven brothers all of questionable I.Q. Although Kenny remained a hopeless fighter, he became an expert archer with words, hitting people in places they never knew existed, puncturing their egos, and sometimes even touching their souls with words so poisonous his victim would wither and not recover. Paul Jones was one of these victims. By the end of the semester, Paul fell from the class Romeo to the class dork as a result of Kenny's attack and the whole class went along with it. We all ignored Paul as he stumbled around in the lower depths of our intricate grading system. Only Kenny didn't ignore him. He continued to tease him. He liked teasing the rodents, which is what he called the weaker kids. He also was fearless in selecting his victims. Once he went off into a tirade of insults he didn't care how many there were or how big they were. Soon it was happening so often, it was tiring. Sometimes it seemed that Kenny wanted to get beaten up.

It was not enough that Kenny was torturing the family with his blasted barrel, he also decided to revive our childhood pact, telling me there was no doubt that I would be elected this year's Indian princess because he was going to follow me over the edge in his barrel. Like a mad man, he insisted that I should pick out my dress right away, as if that would validate his suicidal barrel attempt to conquer the Falls.

"This is the land of the American blonde, Kenny. I'm too Asian to win."

"I'm telling you, pick out your dress – I'll help you pick it out."

"You're insane. I'm not spending money for a dress I'll never wear."

"You're going to win. I know it – I'm sure of it."

"Why? Why are you so sure?"

"Come on, Mei Li," Kenny's voice was purring like a cat. "Don't you remember when we could turn the whole forest into the hoards of the mighty Ghengis Khan, and the trees actually moved across the land? You've got to help me here. Look, I've no intention of dying, but I'm going to do this. And I need you behind me. If you believe you're going to win, then I'll win too."

"You're not going over the Falls, Kenny. You can't be serious."

"I am, Mei Li, I am. Whether I die or not, I'm going over. Now, are you going to help me or are you going to let me die?"

"Kenny, stop it."

"No, we can make this happen."

At first, I tried laughing at him. No one could alter the future. It was as impossible as changing the path of Niagara, or stopping the sands in the hour glass in *The Wizard of Oz*. But little by little I began to believe, and I became both frightened and hopeful at the same time. I was torn between my impulse to save Kenny by destroying the barrel, and my desire to be elected the town's Indian princess. As the barrel continued to be constructed my confidence grew until near the end of my senior year I believed I could win. I wanted to win. I went out and bought a dress. Somehow the construction of the barrel and my winning were connected in my mind, so that instead of stopping my brother as I knew I should, I convinced myself that building a barrel was good therapy for his fallen ego. It was something to make up for not going to college and wasting his life as a tour guide. Meanwhile I kept the dress in a box under my bed instead of in the closet. It was a beautiful dress – not white, but scarlet. It was Asian styled and it was very much like the dress my mother used to wear gambling. I kept it folded under my bed like a blood knot with the devil. Yes, I wanted to be the princess of Niagara.

A week before graduation I deposited my ballot in the school's main hall before going down to the cafeteria. Everybody was nervous. The entire high school voted for the best girl in the senior class to be the Indian princess, sort of like Niagara's Miss America. She didn't have to be the prettiest – last year Pamela Tyler won just because everybody liked her so much – but that was rare. It was usually based more on looks than talent. Marsha Gibson, the class blonde, had been in the rest room all morning throwing up, and Terry Schwartz, a black-haired beauty, was in full make-up today. Every girl harbored a small hope that by some dumb stroke of luck she would be the winner; except for me, I knew I was going to win. I knew because all day the roar of the Falls had been pounding in my ears.

The reason why I won was not because I was beautiful, not because of the barrel, or because I was the best swimmer the school had ever seen. It was because Bobby was the school's football hero and I happened to be the girl he liked. Everyone thought we made the ideal couple. Life can be so ordinary sometimes. What I didn't know was that for the past couple of months my insane brother had been canvassing the school to get me the vote. Kenny could be very charming and insistent when he wanted to. At parties he was always the center of female attention because he was a great dancer, not to mention a big gossip. When it came to dancing, I was the wall flower often sitting on the sidelines with Bobby, who also had two left feet, while Kenny undulated across the floor with Terry Schwartz acting like a bitch in heat in front of him.

So, weeks later after endless rehearsing (there were a lot of awards to be given out), I found myself being pulled in a canoe full of red tulips and yellow roses towards the edge of Niagara Falls, all to the heavy beat of the tomahawk drum corps.

Never before had the pounding roar of the Falls sounded so great – due less to the fact that the entire school drum corps marched behind me than to my state of mind. When Bobby lifted me effortlessly out of the canoe the pounding didn't stop. Lightning crackled along the river, and a cold wet wind rose up out of the Falls. It was joined by the great west wind that rides out of the plains, across the lakes, and was capable of changing the first day of May into what felt like mid-winter. The sky darkened, as the sun pulled the clouds across its face in terror, while thunder rolled across the heavens. For sure, the giant of the Falls had remembered the promise I had made in my childhood that I would stay in the canoe and ride to my death. He was commanding me to get back in the canoe.

Enraged, he tore the plastic decorations down, throwing them onto people's lawns and up into the trees. He snatched people's hats and twisted their hair into bizarre hair-dos. Neither I nor my Indian princesses-in-waiting had coats, so we huddled together while the men tried to put up the tents they had standing by for just such a storm. However, instead of looking prepared they looked even more ridiculous. The minute they tied down one flap, the wind would loosen another, making it billow and flounder like a gigantic white flag, but I would not surrender. In spite of the fat drops of rain, I went to the platform to watch the canoe make the last leg of its journey without me.

Instead of a happy occasion, the whole affair was turning into a nightmare. As they lowered the canoe down into the water, I thought of an empty coffin being lowered into its watery grave. Frightened at being on its own, the canoe twisted dangerously in the current. The wind ripped away the yellow roses, throwing red tulips into the black water, as if looking for something that wasn't there, while the drums continued to pound out their needy demand for sacrifice. The pounding told me I was cheating the Falls by not staying in the canoe as the myth demanded, and my classmates knew it. I was going to be punished. While the sky blackened with rain their faces grew white and their voices shrill as they pushed me towards the water, screaming and pointing. Looking at their open mouths and white teeth, I knew that they were coming to bite and chew my flesh, rip the meat off my bones. I knew it and the funny thing was, I wasn't afraid. Far from it, closing my eyes, I surrendered in a moment of ecstasy. Men were yelling, running towards me with ropes and large hooks. I stared at them as if from a great distance, when Bobby grabbed me and held me down. I didn't know whether he was trying to smother me or shield me from the pelting rain. The men rushed past us to the water's edge, where all my classmates were helplessly watching the canoe, now on its side, and followed by a makeshift barrel.

Immediately I recognized the barrel as Kenny's basement experiment. The pounding stopped while I watched the barrel overtake the canoe. And as I tried to stop time, all the water in the Falls turned to sand. The sand fell slowly and silently, raising great clouds of dust. In a horrible silence both Kenny and the canoe vanished. I fainted, and for the second time that day Bobby had to carry me. When the roar of Niagara returned it sounded hollow and flat. Never again would I speak to Niagara. Never again would I ask for the energy to win a swimming match or anything else. No, the Falls no longer held any magic. It was no longer beautiful. It was the house of the evil spirit.

Blackness descended. The snake had struck. No one had noticed the venomous newborn snake crawling out of the cracked shell of Kenny's ego. It bit everyone in the family. A lantern went out in my mother's eyes. She spent all her time in the casino. The poison immediately drained the energy out of my world, leaving it the dingy color of dirty spring snow. And my father's shoulders stooped even further in sadness and defeat.

It was in the newspaper and on TV. Somebody was videotaping the parade and they ended up taping Kenny's last journey instead. We saw it over and over, the barrel tumbling and turning down the river in the pouring rain. All I could think of was Kenny, clutching his knees, spinning round and round, and waiting to drop out of existence. They never found the body. They found the smashed barrel, but that was all, and they stopped looking, except for Dad. He wouldn't stop. Every day he went out. As long as his legs worked he would walk the river, looking for his son. I couldn't stand the idea of him poking around the ruined rocks and garbage for proof of Kenny's death. I didn't want to see the twisted cartilage and smashed skull he would finally drag home.

After the funeral, Bobby came to say good-bye. He did not get a football scholarship so he was going to take up his uncle's offer of a car dealership in San Bernardino, California. I cried. I cried and cried some more, because my life was over, because Kenny was dead and now Bobby was going away too and I was going to be all alone. I cried until Bobby asked me to marry him. I guess he figured that was the only thing that was going to make me stop crying.

When I left Niagara, the magic of the Falls had vanished. They sounded dull, a slightly fatal tone. Maybe it was just growing up: when you're young you think you hear bells and songs; now that so much had happened, it was just a lot of water pouring over the edge. All I could see were vending machines and wedding motels and signs advertising what used to be there. There was even talk of a new plant that would shut down half of the Falls, maybe even all of it in the summer. That would be funny – the world's greatest falls without water. I didn't care. I never wanted to see the Falls again, but how do you stop your dreams when a hundred pine trees gallop behind you, as you follow the river to rescue your brother from the great city of falling water? How do you forget, when every night you stand before your faithful army of trees and tell them they must prepare to die in order to defeat the giant who has taken back your brother, bringing winter to the land and darkness to the sky, allowing the cold wind to pierce your heart and freeze it in your chest?

8

The car dealer's wife

LIFE WITH BOBBY is not what I expected – I don't know what I expected. The neighborhood Bobby and I have moved into sucks. All of San Bernardino sucks, for that matter. I try to comfort myself with the idea that my new neighborhood is ugly because I'm unhappy, like the fairy princess whose surrounding countryside mirrored her moods, but without the sound of Niagara I do not feel like a princess anymore, I feel like an asshole. So, I'm happy my neighborhood sucks, yes indeed. After all, was my neighbor's newly sprouting lawn, perfectly trimmed Chinese maple trees, shiny red sports car next to the trusty BMW, and God knows how many children all with the latest fashion sportswear, one sneaker of which cost more than any dress in my closet, supposed to cheer me up? I don't think so. I grab the groceries out of the car and drag them inside.

Our tiny house is very clean. That is what happens when you have a lot of spare time on your hands. You clean and organize. You try to regain control and you clean some more. I start to organize the groceries. I don't remember buying this shit: three boxes of Mallomars, a head of lettuce, two gigantic bottles of Vodka, and I forgot to buy dinner. Why bother with dinner anyway? Everyone knows the quickest way to a man's heart is an open chest wound. I rationalize. I can't see wasting that much money on an organ as small as a taste bud. Besides I'm not a good cook. My favorite spice is sugar, nasty little high, and cheap too. You really feel loved munching on a Winchell's donut, and five minutes later you're in an argument. If no one is around to argue with, you're on the phone with your girlfriend, "Hello, Alice? You're a cow. I know you're not screwing my husband – I think you're a cow anyway." I go through girlfriends like toilet paper. Every girl I make friends with gets a crush on my good-looking husband. They all want to fuck him. It's like saliva, they can't control it. They start talking too much, asking where he is. And they all smile that stupid insincere grin. I pick up the phone again, ready to make another lethal pass at Alice. Obviously I'm a little out of control here. Instead, I pull out the vacuum. The vacuum is my friend. The noise reminds me of Niagara when you're very close. So, I have a good cry.

Leaving the vacuum on I sink down on the couch. My eyes close and I can hear the water rushing by. I am inside the barrel turning and spinning as the river carries me along. I curl up with my knees almost touching my chest. I can't stretch my legs out. With every breath, I know there is less air as the roar of Niagara descends on me. I am helpless – my mind filling with the incomprehensible descent before me. Waking up, I turn off the vacuum just in time. The vacuum is not my friend. I pick it up and put it in the trash. I miss Kenny.

I did make this one new friend in the park, a young mother. She drank too, carried a bottle of Stoli in her kid's stroller. We got along great, mainly because she was too loaded to get a crush on Bobby. Every day we sat in the playground and got looped. In the summer, we went to the beach and got so loaded we lost her kid. While I went swimming she passed out and the baby crawled away like a little misguided crab towards the ocean. When I came back, the beach was empty, and she was hysterical. I told her to check the other people on the beach to see if they saw the kid, while I checked the water. Walking through the surf, I didn't really want to find the child. If I did it would be too late. He would be floating face down with a seaweed collar around his neck.

I thought of my Dad looking for Kenny's body every day. I know he didn't want to find it, but he couldn't stop looking. Why? What would it prove if he found it? That Kenny was dead? I knew Kenny was dead. I was always too late. He always died just before I got there. We must have rehearsed it a million times when we were kids, but still I didn't stay in the doomed canoe of flowers as it twisted and spun in its effort to avoid its destiny. The lifeguard called me over. Someone picked the baby up before he could reach the ocean. He was OK . . . just a bad case of sunburn but after that, my friend said she couldn't see me anymore.

The Mexican gang who think they rule our neighborhood have been stealing things off my precious car — first it was my battery, then my hubcaps, and my scoop, and finally my radio. My radio was the last straw. Instead of whining to Bobby, I decided to handle it myself.

Walking into the small bar where the gang hung out, I immediately felt sorry for its customers instead of angry at them. The place was tiny and meticulously painted brown, mismatched chairs and tables were scattered about like broken toys, the jukebox was a boom box and the pool table was the size of a postage stamp. The two or three old men there did not look up from their drinks the whole time I was there, and the four young boys playing pool stood in suspended motion waiting for me to leave. When I explained that I was the owner of the Trans Am, they came to life, very congenially explaining how a woman shouldn't own a car like that. I have to say, I could see their point; it was a macho car, something Bobby had bought for me because it was a good deal, certainly not because it was my kind of car. But still, it was the only car I had. I had become extremely attached to it, and did not want to give it up. Certainly not to a gang of Mexicans. It wasn't until I uttered the word "Mexicans" that I realized I was screaming. Instead of being offended the boys smiled slyly to each other and the leader put down his pool cue, offering me a drink. The smirk on his face suggested that he knew I couldn't pass up a drink, that I was an alcoholic and the whole neighborhood talked about it.

So much for my great plan of attack. I ran out of the bar and back to the shelter of my marriage, but I didn't tell Bobby. He has no idea that I drink all day. I can't believe he doesn't notice. It's annoying. He's either too stupid to notice or too nice to suspect. All Bobby and I do is fuck. It's the only thing that's better than alcohol.

We don't talk much but the minute he kisses me I open up like a clam under steam exposing its most vulnerable muscle. The only time I am happy is when his dick is pushing into me. If I had to say anything positive about my husband it would have to be that he was a good lover, a really good lover. Maybe all dull people are good in bed; that's their compensation for not trying to understand that there is nothing to understand. I, on the other hand, am painfully aware that I think too much, which is why I have such trouble coming. It's so easy for him . . . probably because he is in love with me. Maybe I'm jealous of my husband. Maybe it's much more fun to be in love than be loved by someone? Maybe I think too much?

I am interrupted by a loud knocking at the front door, "Oh great, another intrusion." Opening up, I'm shocked to find two of the Mexican boys from the bar, just standing there, staring insolently at me. When I try to shut the door, they pull out what looks like maybe two hundred dollars and assure me that they have only come to buy my car. The one doing the talking is older and his eyes travel intimately over my body as he speaks to me.

"It's not for sale."

"Two hundred dollars and we get you a nice car."

"No, I like the one I have. I don't want a stolen car."

"But lady, your car is a man's car. We can get you a lady's car. What do you want, a Toyota?"

I slam the door in his face. The nerve of those little bastards. The only place I feel safe is in my car, which is why my car trips are becoming more and more extensive. If I don't do something to curb my little car trips, I will be grocery shopping in San Francisco and Las Vegas for the barest necessities . . . now, where was I? My hands run down my body to their familiar place between my legs. Oh yes . . . when I can feel Bobby's dick entering me, blind, abrupt, and over-eager — yes, I love his dick, it's the rest of him that I have a problem with. I forgave the third member of our bedroom romance all of his faults. As a matter a fact, I enjoyed the simple appetites of his dick, the fact that he couldn't stop once he got going, and then after he had spit up every ounce of sperm he could muster, after that small but incredible show, the way he fell down shrunken from exhaustion and effort . . .

Forget it. Jerking off is too much work. Rolling over on the couch I stare at the ceiling. It's at this point that I reach for the bottle of vodka hidden behind the vacuum. We have a bottle on the bar, but I never drink from that. Fuck these fucking Mexicans. A few more slugs from the vodka bottle and I'm ready to show the fucking neighborhood who was fit to drive a Trans Am. Totally loaded, it takes me an hour to find the damn keys. But when I do there's no stopping me.

I get in the car, turn on the motor, put my foot on the gas, and nothing. The car doesn't move. Okay, let's go over this. It can't be the battery. Right, the motor is running. Slamming it into reverse, I gun it, and still the car won't move. A crowd accumulates around the car to watch me. I'll give them a show, I'll run them over. Throwing the gears back into drive, I floor it, making the motor scream, but all the car does is shake peculiarly. Through the windshield I can see smirks on the faces of the Mexican gang watching me in my aquarium. Great, my worst nightmare, I look like a fool in broad daylight . . . It has to be a dream, but I can't wake up. Getting out of the car in a rage, I slam the door as hard as I can and concentrate on walking away. Their laughter snickers at my heels like stray dogs.

Turning around to face my tormentors, I notice that my car is sitting on blocks. All four wheels have been stolen. I was trying to drive without wheels and, of course, no one told me. No one said, "Hey, your wheels are missing." No, they just stood by and thought, "I want to see this drunken bitch drive that Trans Am right off its blocks."

The sky went black, just like it was night, only it was still day, and I thought, an eclipse. That's funny. I didn't hear anything about it on the TV. But then, who can hear anything with all that laughing going on. The crowd pushed around me as lightning crackled along the river. Like a leper I walked through the crowd and they scattered before me. If I could just make it to my door . . .

Inside . . . thank God.

The next day the entire car is missing and I have to tell Bobby. I'm so angry, I end up screaming at Bobby, who doesn't seem to be that concerned about the whole thing. "I want those little bastards put in jail before I get another car."

"They're your neighbors. You don't even know it's them. Why didn't you let me handle this?"

"They're fucking shit, that's what they are. They're as bad as Indians. If my dad knew I was living in a neighborhood like this – "

"Why are you so angry? The car's insured."

"I'm not angry. I don't give a shit if it's insured."

"I'll get you a new one. I'm a car dealer, remember?

I'll get you something nobody's going to steal, like a Volkswagon."

"I don't want a Honda or a stupid Volkswagon or any of that shit."

Bobby grabs me and pulls me to him. "Molly, shut up. You're losing it. It's just a car."

Pressed up against his chest all my anger reorganizes itself into another more powerful drive whose focus point is Bobby. I want to fuck him. We start in and end up doing it on the couch. When it's over with my body half buried under his, I get my reward. I feel at peace. Closing my eyes I can see the silver river before me glittering in the afternoon sun. If only I could swim in it, I would be happy, but I cannot. The tapping of the hammer has already started.

9

Going home

❦

THE NEXT MORNING I was in the middle of my customary breakfast of vodka and tonic, when the aimless drifting of my life in California suddenly took on the direction of a rushing river and all because of a yellow piece of paper. It was a telegram from Ma: "YOUR FATHER HAS DIED COME HOME." Those six words unblocked a river that only flowed one way, north, back to the Falls. I was going home.

On the plane I tried to imagine what Niagara would sound like this time. As a child I thought that I would always hear Niagara pounding in the distance. I couldn't imagine a moment without it. When we went to visit Grandma in Buffalo I felt like a child without a heartbeat. The strange silence made me anxious until we returned home where the sound once again kept me company, reassuring me that I was never alone. But that was then. Now that I had been away so long, I didn't know how I would feel hearing Niagara again.

There was another sound I didn't want to hear: the sound of my mother's voice. Although my dad would call often to check up on his little girl even if he didn't have anything to say, Ma never called. Because of her accent she mistrusted the phone. Even for something as personal as death, she chose to send a formal telegram. It had been a year and a half since I talked to her, and as far as I was concerned, it wasn't long enough.

Perhaps that is why, when I got there, I couldn't bring myself to go home right away. Instead I went to the old tree house where Kenny and I played as kids. Back then the tree house was capable of transforming into a castle turret or a basement dungeon depending on our mood. But no matter what room the oak tree took on, it stood so close to the Falls that the sound of water was its permanent wallpaper. It was under this wallpaper that I first had sex. The insides of the oak had been blackened and burnt out by lightning, while the outside, by some miracle, was still alive and producing green leaves every spring. When I lay down inside it, it was as if I had crawled inside nature herself to sleep. Closing my eyes, I listened to the choir of the leaves as they sang over the deeper symphony of water. The sound was fainter that day because the wind was to the west.

High school had started and Kenny's club house friends wanted to sit around with real girls instead of dirty magazines. So, when the club house was empty, I retook it with a vengeance. I used it as my hiding place to bring boys to. Now I was popular, not Kenny. I smoked cigarettes in the warm sun after swimming with the boys and I drank beer in the late afternoon with them and when the sun went down I would decide which one could kiss me or not. At first Kenny was furious that his friends would rather be with me. But there was only one boy I was interested in.

He was late. I didn't know whether to torment him or forgive him right away, letting those moody lips find my own, or make them smile as I toyed with the buttons of his shirt. Anxiously, I waited for him. Beside me lay the unopened letters I found in his room. They were from colleges, all of them far away. He was going to leave me, and I had to do everything in my power to make him stay.

I heard him coming through the dried leaves, dead secrets erupting into life with every footfall. He was running, but he couldn't outrun the rattle of the leaves. I didn't move. I lay there waiting until I felt his fingers on my exposed ankles, along my legs, and then he was beside me, his heart pounding alongside Niagara's distant rumble.

"I didn't surprise you, did I?"

"I heard you coming."

"You're not happy to see me?"

"Here," I handed him the letters, and he looked away, staring out of the great crack in the tree with that faraway look he used when we played our adult version of house. At first, I wondered what he saw, but he didn't see anything. He didn't want to see. He was brooding inward on his own imaginary landscape. Rolling over on my back, my eyes crossed the blue satin pillow of sky and came to his marble face with its green eyes half closed. This would mean the snake was asleep – the spiteful snake that was coiled around the base of his backbone – and we could laugh. His laughter was different now, full of sadness instead of sarcasm. I was never sure if I understood the joke but I always laughed when he laughed. The pleasure was all in watching him.

"You didn't open them," I persisted.

He stared at the letters. "I know. I don't want to."

"Then I will." I tore open the letters and read them, "Oh Kenny, all these colleges have accepted you, New York, Boston, even California. You might as well be going to Alaska."

I watched his mouth, waiting for him to speak. My favorite part, if I had to pick one, was his mouth. Kenny's mouth was the entrance of the cave where his tongue slept, and I watched this entrance all the time when I was little. It was a game we played; if I saw the tongue animal stick its tip out of its cave I could get a wish, but the tongue was afraid of noise so I had to be very quiet. In this way Kenny got his little sister to sit quietly for hours staring patiently at his mouth.

Later when I lay on my stomach dreaming of the tongue animal sleeping in its pink cave, I would get the urge to coax it out of its wet lair. First I thought of giving it a name and calling it, but tongues don't have ears. Then I tried to think of what kind of food I might lure the sightless creature with, when it suddenly dawned on me that the best way would be to use my own tongue to separate Kenny's smile and . . . A buzz vibrated my body. I was thinking of a kiss. I sat bolt upright but the dream didn't vanish. It hung in the air. It took up all the space in my brain. That's when I first knew I wanted to kiss my older brother.

Perhaps if we had never kissed things would have been simpler; I would have been sad all semester, and then happy at Christmas and spring break when he returned. But now things were not that easy. I whispered in his ear that my heart would break when he left. It would explode in anger over the sophisticated girls he would meet at college, and I dreaded the day he would return to treat me just as a sister again . . . like nothing happened . . . like I didn't matter.

"But I'm not going," he said quietly. I caught my breath, unable to believe my luck as Kenny continued in a matter of fact voice, "I've already got a job. I'm staying here till you graduate."

Of course, I should have said, Oh no, you have to go to college, but I knew it would have sounded as fake as a talking flounder. It was all I could do to suppress the victory in my voice. "What job?"

"On the sightseeing boat for Niagara. I'm a guide."

I put my arms around his skinny shoulders and kissed him. His green eyes went black like the grass under a thundercloud. His feelings moved across his eyes like the clouds across the sky, throwing threatening shadows along the green grass. Sometimes I wasn't sure I understood him, other times, I didn't care so long as he loved me.

"Kenny," I said, "let's make love."

"We can't, it's not right."

"We don't have the same mother."

"We have the same father."

"No one's going to know. You do love me, don't you?"

"It's not just that, you're under-age. I'd be thrown in jail."

It all sounded so dramatic. "You do love me, don't you," I insisted.

"Yes, but – "

"Is there someone else?"

"No." Kenny dropped his head in his hands. He looked so tormented, so beautiful.

"Molly, you save that stuff for your boyfriend."

"I don't want anyone else. I want you. Come on, Kenny, lie down with me. I know you want to."

"You must never tell anyone, Mei Li." I helped him take off my blouse.

Was I aware that I was a terrible flirt? If I was, I didn't know where I got it from, certainly not from my mother. Except for playing cards she never did anything sexy, and if I did, she yelled at me, close your bathrobe, lower your eyes, close your mouth. Once I was parading around in a scarf wrapped like a sarong. Dad was laughing at me, saying to Ma, "Look, she looks like you used to," when my mother's face went black with anger. After that I started calling her Dragon Lady to her face. She refused to let me wear a bikini, me, the swimming champion. And as for bras, she went ballistic when she found me wearing one. You'd think they were the cause of the Western decline. I had to hide mine in my knapsack and put it on in the school bathroom.

"Do you want to break all the muscles and have breasts like cow udders? By the time you're thirty you'll have to get plastic ones like every one else."

"Ma, they get plastic tits because they like them. Men like big tits here."

"Don't talk back to me. You're too smart for your own good."

She was definitely the kind of mother that could fuck up a girl's sex drive. At times I wondered if I was adopted. I was sure that Ma didn't have sex. Dad and she were so immersed in their own separate addictions, drinking and gambling, they barely seemed to talk, much less kiss. They were like the sun and the moon, never in the same place at the same time. Dinner was the only time they saw each other. Ma would wake up and come out of her room dressed and freshly made up just as Dad wandered home rumpled and drunk from his afternoon visit to the local bars. After dinner she would put on her lucky gold coin earrings and go to the casino while Dad helped us with our homework or went to his room to drink some more.

I lay naked on the ground waiting for Kenny. He was fumbling with the buckle of his jeans, whispering in a hurried voice. "If we do it, you must never do it with anyone else.

"I know."

"Especially Bobby."

"He just kisses me, nothing else."

Kenny lowered his body on mine. "How does he kiss you?"

"On the mouth, with his mouth open."

"Tell me what he does."

"He comes real close with his lips apart, and if I don't do anything he makes this little noise."

"Go on."

"Then we kiss."

"How? Tell me how you kiss."

"I don't know. He never closes his mouth. He's like a fish. He doesn't need air and his tongue moves like he's talking . . . and he makes noises like he's hurt . . ." I stopped. Kenny was inside me.

"Go on. What's he do with his hands?"

Kenny came quickly and we hurriedly put our clothes back on as if we couldn't talk until we were fully clothed. It wasn't the perfect union I imagined from the movies. Instead of being with him where time and space melted for one moment – I was alone. It was very sobering to learn that little piece of loneliness was what the big mystery of sex was all about, and for the first time I agreed with my English literature teacher: "Ode to a Grecian Urn" was correct; wanting sex was much more thrilling than getting it.

Although I would never admit it, the best part wasn't sex, it was lying next to Kenny, getting high, and listening to music with only a fraction of my skin, an elbow or a knee, burning into a fraction of his skin. The intensity of that fraction was forever burnt into my brain. All of the CDs Kenny had collected had to be hidden in the tree house because of Dad. Show tunes and fashion magazines were trash to our macho-minded father, since the only thing he believed in was hunting and sports. He was forever threatening to take Kenny on a hunt, but he never did because the first time he threw out all of Kenny's records, Kenny said he would shoot him.

I sort of understood Dad for throwing out the glossy art and fashion magazines. They intimidated him. They intimidated me too because I didn't like art the passionate way that Kenny did, and although I never let on, when Kenny would leaf through an art magazine and talk of us going to New York or LA, I secretly dreaded leaving Niagara. There was a blank spot in Kenny that I was afraid of because if it was filled with something I didn't understand, I knew I would lose him. And there was that sad way he would stare into space forever when we were alone. He wasn't like Bobby, whose every thought I knew long before he said it and sometimes I even had to help him express it. Kenny was different. I could never tell what was in his head. But what did it matter, as long as I could hear the rushing of Niagara alongside Kenny's beating heart.

10

The Beard

WHEREVER MY SEXUAL appetite came from, all the moves came naturally to me at a very young age. If my high school had had any imagination I would have played Salome in the school play. But out here, in the woods of the Northeast, where the largest city is named after a buffalo, theater was not an important part of the school curriculum. We were encouraged to settle for cheerleading instead. I refused. I did not think there was anything sexy or dramatic about calisthenics and I told them if they needed a spectacle, I would rather be crucified in the middle of the football field naked than be forced to jump up and down in a very short skirt so guys could see my underwear. It was heartfelt remarks like this that got me the reputation of being defiant.

What the puritan Northeast did have was a rather rigid sense of decency, and Kenny and I would have been stoned if it were not for Bobby. He was the perfect beard. Since he was always with us, everybody assumed that Bobby and I were a couple. The school football hero had to have a girlfriend and I was it, that's how they think in the great Northeast. Thanks to my expert combo of cock-tease and flirt, Bobby thought we were going together too.

The whole charade was pretty easy to pull off because no one really dated in high school. We did everything in groups, like a little pack of wolves. We would all pile into two or three cars and caravan into the next high school's territory for a dance or just to invade their greasy spoon or bowling ally. Those long night drives on beer and cigarettes with the music blaring were as erotic as dancing close and much easier to arrange. With our bodies smashed together we would fly over the country roads, hitting sixty on the bumps called Thank You Ma'ams so the car lifted off the ground, or we'd turn out the lights and drive blind to our favorite CDs.

Once in enemy territory, we would drink some more and look for trouble, which consisted of acting really tough and waiting for something to happen, some insult, some minor infraction of the code, or for someone to call someone out. If it happened to be Kenny, which quite often it was, Bobby would step in as the gladiator. The drama spread like a brush fire as the other school matched Bobby with their own quarterback. After a sufficient amount of insult trading everyone loaded up in their cars again. This time there would be as many as eight or nine cars because there would always be onlookers, even adults. After all, small towns could be pretty boring and going to a good fight was standard entertainment.

The caravan of cars disappeared into the nearest field or vacant lot outside of town. A circle would be drawn in the moonlight and after even more drinking, Bobby and the other boy would take off their shirts, and circle one another before squaring off to fight. The sexual excitement of these fights was so intense that the one or two rock concerts I got to see seemed like garden parties in comparison. The cheers of the audiences sounded fake compared to the high-pitched screams of the girls standing around the dirt circle. Maybe it was the moon glowing on the white skin of the fighters that made the girls totally lose it, screaming encouragement of the lewdest kind while the boys pressed up against them from behind, their own eyes glazed by the promise of blood.

Kenny would be in a frenzy, acting like Bobby's manager, coach, and mother all rolled into one. But in fact, he was more of a nuisance than anything else. When the two fighters entered the ring there was no room for anyone else. I never yelled or heckled at these events like some of these girls who squealed like stuck pigs. Instead, I stood at the edge of the ring watching in cold formality as if I were the high priestess, the shark inside me staring out of my eyes. Before every fight Bobby and I would lock eyes and from that moment on, my eyes never left him. "Bring me blood, Bobby," was all they said. Bobby would kiss the air between us and then turn and do as he was told.

Bobby wasn't that aggressive in the ring, which added to the tension. He was always getting hit first. It was as if he couldn't fight unless the other guy hit him. Sometimes he would get really pounded until out of nowhere, his body would uncoil and the other boy would be bleeding and staggering, trying to figure out what hit him. Blood was the only thing that satisfied our frenzy. It is one of the most precious sights I keep locked in the memory bank: the blood on Bobby's hands as he backed away from his stunned opponent, and then uncoiled, and opened up the guy's face a second time, along with the screams of my classmates and the smell of everyone's excitement.

After each fight, I always kissed Bobby. I would kiss him and lick the sweat off his face just to see Terry Schwartz's eyes swim in jealousy. All the girls in my class thought he was a dreamboat. But when I was alone with him, I couldn't see it. He was good-looking but his neck was too thick. His young body was too muscled for my taste. His shoulders and arms stretched out his tee-shirt while his blue jeans looked like they were going to fall off. His face was beautifully chiseled, but he had those thick curvy lips like you see on Greek statues, lips that old men want and only young boys have. I thought they were puffy.

Still it was fun making the girls in my class jealous, girls I never really got along with because they wanted something and I would never give it to them. If they couldn't fuck Bobby then they wanted me to.

The same girls, who thought Bobby was a knock-out, were always teasing me about when I was going to do it with him. By the time senior year rolled around, they grew disappointed and angry at my inability to consummate their idea of a perfect couple. They labeled me the class prude not to be included in their sex gossip, which was extensive, since most of the girls were in bed with someone. I even suspect they elected me to be the virgin Indian princess as a warning instead of an honor. I understood the pressure; heroes got laid and if I didn't have sex with Bobby, the class couldn't relax. If it wasn't for my affair with Kenny, I would have folded long ago, but instead I defied them. It was no wonder I imagined them an angry mob rearing up on its hind legs to rip me apart the day of the parade.

But I was impervious to their attacks and my secret was Kenny. Our incestuous affair made me feel superior; if fucking and swimming were anything alike I was farther out than any of my round-eyed classmates ever dared to go. As for the boys in the class, they unjustly labeled me a cock-tease, which in our young TV brains carried the same shame that "adulterer" did for the Pilgrims when they first landed. But I didn't take this seriously. It didn't seem to stop them from vying to be the first ones onto my virgin shores.

Determined to have their way, the class insisted on throwing us together. At the state fair we presided, and for the May dance, we were elected king and queen, not to mention all the football rallies. I was always kissing Bobby in public, but in private, it was a different story. He had this insistent hard-on that he eagerly pressed against any part of my body he could. It pissed me off and I used to tell him so.

"Damn it, Bobby, keep your tongue in your mouth or I'll bite it off next time."

Bobby grins as if my threat could be considered just another more bizarre form of sex. "Hey, we're going together, aren't we? What's wrong with – "

"I'm not some piece of wood you get to jerk off on."

Bobby's smile vanished, "I'm not getting off. I'm just kissing you."

"You make me feel cheap."

"Cheap?"

"You know what I mean."

"No, I don't."

"I'm just telling you to keep your tongue in your mouth."

"Damn it, Molly, maybe we shouldn't be going together. I just don't understand you."

"What's that supposed to mean?"

"I don't think you like me."

"Bobby, if you're going to tell me I have to fuck you in order to prove that I like you, I don't – "

"Shut up. I'm not saying that. I don't want you to prove anything. I just want to know that you feel – shit, you always make it sound like I – "

"I'm not doing the talking, you are."

"And I'm not asking you to get pregnant. I'm just asking you to return my kiss."

"And then one thing leads to another."

"No, no, it doesn't. The fact is you don't want to kiss me. I can feel it. Sometimes I think I'm going crazy. You like your own brother more than me."

"Bobby." I sounded so shocked and hurt, my performance amazed even me. "Do you know what you're saying? He's my brother. Of course I love him. But I don't love him like that."

"I don't mean it like that. Shit, I can't even talk to you. I don't know. Maybe we should split up."

"Bobby, look me in the eye. I love you but I'm not going to do anything until I'm married. If you want to go with Terry Schwartz or Marsha or all the fucking cheerleaders and get laid, I'll understand. But I don't want to fuck around. I only want to do it for real."

"I don't want Terry or anyone else. I love you." The more I told him to go, the more doggedly he followed me.

"Then come here and kiss me." This is what I really

loved, kissing Bobby and pretending it was Kenny. Bobby's kisses tasted like forbidden fruit, like a guilty pleasure that I couldn't enjoy unless it was for Kenny's sake. The truth was, Bobby was a much better kisser than Kenny. In public, when Bobby had his arms around me and was nibbling my ear while Kenny sat next to us in the same booth, I could feel Kenny watching us, like someone watching a movie, without the slightest bit of jealousy.

To get Bobby to promise to back off the sex until we were married and stop the mouth to mouth resuscitation kissing, I had to stop talking to him, which threw him into a tailspin. That worked. Miserable, to the point of doing something foolish, he promised he would wait for wedding bells . . . and then, I would start kissing him again. His tongue could talk, coaxing, licking and pleading with my tongue to come on out and play, saying what he could never put into words. Before I realized what his tongue was saying I could feel his whole body echoing those words from the surface of my skin deep down into the hidden parts of my body, and the alarm in my head would sound – not in control . . . losing control – this is where I put on the brakes. Kenny was brilliant . . . Bobby was vulgar, and I didn't want to be like him, but there were times when my body wouldn't listen to me.

Whenever Bobby wouldn't do what Kenny and I wanted all I had to do was stop talking to him and he gave in. Sometimes Kenny demanded too much, and I felt sorry for Bobby, but that's how I wanted it. In my little black heart I was guilty. I was leading Bobby on, but it had to be done. As long as Bobby looked like my date, nobody would find out about my brother and me.

No one even suspected. After all, no one in the North-east was a pervert . . . maybe in the degenerate South, or decadent New York City, and God knows, in LA they fucked anything, but the Northeast was an honest and friendly place.

Kenny was late again. He had started going out with the boys late at night. His friends would call him up at eleven or even one o'clock in the morning and he would go meet them somewhere. Ma and he often waited up for each other and ended up talking in her bedroom till dawn. I tried not to be jealous; after all I was the one he was fucking. I couldn't imagine him wanting someone as old as my mother. I couldn't even imagine my mother undressed, much less in a sexual pose. Still, she and Kenny continued to hole up in her bedroom and drive me insane. As always I was powerless against her. If I stayed up to interrupt their bedroom chat, the reception I got was more than chilly. Both of them couldn't wait for me to leave. So, leave I did, to return to my room and curse my mother for horning in where it was obvious she didn't belong.

Nursing the green fire in the pit of my stomach, I pictured her red nails gliding through Kenny's black curls – gliding like the reflection of the moon as it slipped through the dark waters of the night. The red nails trailing down his face like red tears and over his ribs like drops of blood – blood everywhere, as I tore into their white skin, jackknifing in a frenzy of delight. I was swimming again. It was my old shark dream. At last I had fallen asleep only to be awakened by a scream from Ma. It sounded as if someone was ripping the flesh off her bones.

I ran downstairs in time to see Ma trying to drag Kenny's body over the threshold. She lifted his face into the light and blood poured down his chin, staining his shirt. It was real blood. His nose was smashed and his lip and eye were cut. One eye was turning purple, and there were other bruises all over his face. As I helped her drag him inside I heard a car drive away. Whoever had done this to him knew him because they had also driven him home.

It was my dad who patched Kenny up. He did it without a word while Ma cried and wrung her hands. I cried also, but mostly because she was crying. I hated her for crying. Kenny was mine and I felt I was the only one who had a right to cry. Then my jealousy turned on my father as I hungrily watched him touch my lover. It was the most tender thing I had ever seen him do. His thick clumsy hands were at once delicate and deft, so that you could see how familiar he was with bar room brawls. He washed and bandaged his son's cuts, checked his teeth to see how loose they were, his ribs to see if they were broken and his knuckles to see if they were split. And then he straightened his nose out. Whenever Kenny winced he would smile, patting him affectionately. The cold green fire that I had never been able to control from the very first time I saw Kenny smoldered between my ribs. For tonight, and tonight alone Kenny was my father's child, the son he always wanted, and there was nothing Ma or I could do about it.

The next day I got a little satisfaction when Kenny told me he had fought over me.

"Tell me, Kenny. Tell me what happened."

"This guy in a bar said something insulting and I had to punch him out." Kenny tilted his head as he examined his new look in the mirror. It looked like his opponent did most of the punching.

"Kenny, that's terrible." His words were like water, reducing my green fire to gray steam. My gut returned to its familiar cold and blackened state as I waited for more details. "Who was it?"

"A schmuck from the visiting team. I suppose he's got the hots for you. He said some things and I let him have it."

"We should tell Bobby."

"Don't call Bobby. I don't want him to know about this one."

It was odd that Kenny didn't want Bobby to know but I was so pleased Kenny would fight over me, I didn't pay any attention to it. I was too busy pretending distress instead, "Oh Kenny, this is all my fault. I'm so sorry the schmuck hurt you."

"Don't be. I enjoyed it."

Kenny turned from the mirror and smiled at me, his green eyes glittering from under his swollen black skin. "I saw the dress you bought for the parade. It's beautiful. Will you try it on for me?"

11

Maid of the mist

❧

STARING DOWN AT my father's grave his voice came back to me, ricocheting across the dining room table like a ball bearing rolling around on polished wood. "What's he going to do for the rest of his life? Live at home like a homo, a faggot? Those are the kind of boys who live at home, who never date girls." It always came back to the fact that Kenny would not go out with girls. Ed had gone so far as to set Kenny up with the daughters of his friends, and then the cocktail waitress at the Red Dog lounge who he thought was attractive, and finally, Sally Karnowski, the chubby blonde girl who worked at the Motel Six. What was Ed doing at the Motel Six? May hung her head until her hair touched her food. I stared at my plate too, all the proof in the world of Kenny's sexuality held silently between my legs. I wanted to yell out, "He loves me, that's why he's not dating other girls," but that would have made things even worse. So I had to sit there and do nothing while

Dad beat a dead horse and Kenny's green eyes glittered with hate.

"Sally Karnowski is not a girl. She's a female pig," Kenny snarled back.

"Fine, then get someone else. Bring home a woman, God damn it." Dad was really drunk.

"Why? So you can watch. You're the one who doesn't have a dick anymore."

"It's your crazy mother's fault that you're queer. That's where it comes from."

"Leave my mother out of it, you pathetic drunk."

Dad would go on in a slow boil. "If I'd known, I never would have brought you into this house."

"I never wanted to come here."

"Then get out."

Ma pulled her head up. "No, you can't throw him out. I won't have it." Ma's word was the law, so there would be this long silence until Dad couldn't stand it anymore and he would start in again.

"Why is he always hanging around with that crazy quarter back, Bobby Earlanger? They're both fags, and I don't want them in the house."

"Ed, stop it. Bobby is a nice boy. He'll make a good husband for Molly."

"No. No, he won't," I announced coming out of my stupor. "How can you say that. Are you crazy?"

"Shut up, Mei Li. You're the one who is crazy. You don't even know what's good for you."

I shut my mouth and eyes, concentrating on the dried leaves whispering across the ground, and the pounding of the Falls in the distance, or was that just the blood inside my head?

"A tour guide? What kind of a job is that?" Dad's voice would start again.

All summer Kenny worked on one of the six tour boats called *Maid of the Mist*. It was like one of our childhood games come to life. Every day Kenny was imprisoned on that boat. It frightened and saddened me that he was wasting his life, but it also made me feel like a princess to have a young knight toiling in the rapids for my love. Up the river, past American Falls to Horse Shoe Falls he was forced to tell the same Indian myth over and over to people he hated. It was a myth we grew up with and loved, but now it felt like razor blades were being pulled over his tongue every time he had to tell it. Still, he couldn't pull himself away from me.

"Excuse me, could you tell us that story about the Falls again." Kenny looked down into the plump face of the woman who spawned the very overweight children seated next to her before the giant-bellied man on her other side had stopped fucking her because it was a fleshy impossibility. Maybe blow jobs were still possible, but if he gained any more weight she would run the risk of having her head crushed. Stop it. He had to stop thinking like this. It didn't help. He looked at the little fat family before him in their identical disposable rain-coats like a line of sausage wrapped in plastic skins. They were uncomfortable and they would get more uncomfortable as the boat began to sink in the foam of the Falls. Soon they would be scared to death. He couldn't wait.

"Excuse me, Kenny, isn't that your name? Could you tell us that story again? It's so beautiful."

"Yes ma'am, it's very beautiful, and it happened right here. Every year the Indians sacrificed the most beautiful maiden in the village to the god of the Falls. She was put naked in a canoe, and – "

"Naked! You didn't say that before. You said she was dressed in white buckskin."

"White buckskin is actually an Indian term for naked. They didn't have a word for clothed because they were always naked, and white buckskin meant really naked. It was the missionaries who decided that white buckskin meant clothed because clothing was so important to their moral little hairy brains."

"Oh, that's so interesting. That really makes perfect sense."

"Good. So this beautiful naked girl is made to lie down in a canoe, on a bed of fruit and flowers." Kenny could see the fat man's eyes light up. He was right, the guy hadn't been laid in years. A hand job was all he could hope for, and a stack of dirty magazines. "Then they let the canoe drift towards the Falls, closer and closer." The fat man shifted his weight and Kenny felt the boat move. "But her brother couldn't bear to see his sister die like this, and jumping in his canoe he raced to save her. Just as his canoe reached hers, she went over, and her lover was so heartbroken he let his canoe follow her."

"Her lover? I thought you said it was her brother?"

"I did. In this culture as in the Egyptian culture incest was allowed between brothers and sisters."

"That's disgusting."

"It was commonly done."

"Well, it's a good thing they sacrificed her."

"Mom, shut up, let him tell the story."

Kenny stared at the water. This is what incest does to you, rots your brain, grows hair on your palms – no, that's masturbation. Incest is the sport of the gods. Right, and it's making me act like a condescending bitter god who didn't get to go to Harvard. But then weren't all gods bitter and spiteful?

"So, both her boat and his boat went down, and they drowned together, and the mist that always hangs over the Falls are her tears, and the roar of Niagara is his voice crying in anguish forever, Amen. Oh Jesus Christ – "

"Hey Mister, are you okay? You look sea sick."

"Look, Harry, those people up there are waving to us. Wave back, kids. Aloha. Hi."

But the people weren't waving. They were pointing and motioning to where the body fell.

"Mom, Mom, the boat is sinking."

Kenny ran back to the captain who screamed above the roar, "Kenny, can you see her?"

"Yes. It's too late," screams Kenny as he points to the Falls, "She's going into the eddy." The roar and the spray have become terrifying as the boat sinks lower. It's a combo that has never failed to put fear in his gut no matter how many times he does this, but this time it is different. This time he feels like a hero in a movie. Moving back to the rail he almost laughs at the fat family who are on their knees gripping their seats. "Get as close as you can, but I think it's too late."

"What color is her dress?"

"Red, a red dress. Get closer."

"We can't go any farther."

Racing up to the prow again Kenny yells, "Closer. I know her."

But the captain shakes his head. He can't see. He can

barely open his eyes the spray is so fierce, "There's nothing there. I don't see anything red."

"Closer," Kenny stood with his hands gripping the rail, but he did not jump in. "Like father like son," he whispered, "I am a coward." A coward because the first thing he thought was that the lady in the red dress was me.

At dawn Dad went with a group of men to look for the lady in red. He took his makeshift hooks and poles with him down river, trying to figure out where the Falls would throw her back up. Sometimes the Falls never gave the body back, sometimes it gave back things that it had taken a long time ago, and other times it spit the sacrifice back right away, as if it wasn't good enough. From one Indian princess the sacrifice had gone up to eight suicides and Dad always went on all the searches. It was a job, and he was good at it. It calmed him, reminded him of hunting with his uncles in the woods of Maine. Those had been the happiest times of his life, hunting and listening to his uncles tell stories about World War Two.

They had been three brothers going off to defend their country but only two came back. The youngest one who didn't make it was Eddy's father. Eddy never saw him, which was why the uncles told him so many tales of their younger brother's heroics on the battle-field, that and the fact that they still missed their little brother no matter how many years went by. Of course when Eddy got older he realized that his father couldn't have accomplished all those feats of valor, but it was too late. The damage had been done. On his eighteenth birthday Eddy enlisted in the Marines. Now, as he crawled over the twisted roots and dead trees at the end of his life, he could almost hear and smell the virgin forest of his boyhood. Somewhere here was a body of a lady in a red dress, and he would find her.

The next day the other men gave up the hunt, but Dad continued walking the river. As he searched, the empty motel room she never returned to crept into his mind. There was no luggage, no note, no bus ticket back, just an open phone book on the bed, and . . . wait a minute. Then he saw it: a backward bent fist connected to a smashed arm and a twisted body half snagged on an old uprooted tree. The fist held an open purse robbed of all its contents. Ed shook his head, "Women. Why would someone take a purse on such a journey?"

Dad was proud of being able to find and bring things back from the Falls, but even that was twisted away from him. He never planned on searching for his own son. To everyone's amazement, when Kenny died, Ed stopped drinking. I don't know if he thought it was his fault and he was punishing himself, or if he made a pledge and his drinking was the sacrifice. Every day he went out to look for Kenny's body stone-cold sober. I was the one who started hitting the liquor cabinet in our house. For the second time I waited for Dad to bring me a brother home from under the Falls. Only this time instead of a pale child with black curly hair it would be a sack full of mangled bits of meat.

12

The snow plough

DAD'S FUNERAL WAS miserable compared to my brother's. When Kenny was put to rest the whole school attended. It was even on the news. I was interviewed three times because Dad refused to talk and Ma was too shy about her accent. I felt so important. But now I realize he was just another newspaper clipping to them, another name to go along with Winnie Edison Taylor, George Stalakis, and William Redhill senior and junior.

My poor father, it started snowing halfway through his ceremony. The wind came riding out of the west, screaming like an Indian across the Great Plains and then, magically turning into silent snow, as it passed over the Great Lakes. Maybe this winter the Falls will freeze just for a day or two.

I looked around at the people shivering while the grave was tended to. It wasn't very crowded, a couple of bartenders and my mom looking small and thinner, sandwiched in between two dark-skinned men, with long black hair. They were her only friends, Indians, probably the owners of the new casino that lit up the night as I drove in from the airport, while the giant factories remained dark and empty, pyramids of a dead industry.

One of the bartenders my father was friendly with came up to me and started talking in an effort to relieve the sadness that filled the spaces in between the flakes of snow. "He was a good man, your dad. Always came into my bar. If you would like to come by, drinks are on the house for you."

"Thanks."

"I would really like it if you would come. The bar is a good place. Your dad spent a lot of time there."

"Okay. Sure, I'd be happy to come."

I let my eyes wander over to Kenny's empty grave. Sometimes I hated him for leaving me, for upstaging my poor canoe and its bedraggled flowers. By dying he even robbed me of my hatred, demoting me to a grave-side mourner again. Other times I was consumed with guilt. I blamed myself for his death because I didn't act like a sister. I acted like a jealous lover. Incest never bothered me like it bothered him. The wind shifted, and I heard the sound of the Niagara, faint in the dis-tance, the way it sounded alongside Kenny's heart when I laid my head on his chest. Looking up, I noticed a man standing off to the side of the funeral, partially hidden by a large elm. He reminded me of my brother. I stared at him, until finally he looked at me. When our eyes met, a chill of recognition went through me. He looked away and started walking towards his car. It couldn't have been Kenny, but for that moment I was convinced it was. I started running towards him as he got in a car and drove off. I kept on running, undecided as to whether I wanted to hit him or hug him.

No one stopped me. They probably thought I was grief-stricken and needed to be alone. I did not have to look back to see the bartenders roll their eyes in a "crazy like father like daughter" look, or see my mother shake her head with the corners of her mouth drawn down in disappointment, the old "she couldn't even stay long enough to save face" look. Even though there was no hope of catching the car that was pulling Kenny out of my life again, I kept on running. The cold wind on my face felt good. I wanted it to anesthetize my brain, to freeze all the memories and finally put them to sleep under the blanket of snow. But the little black hole in the white blanket, the little black hole they had buried my father in didn't disappear. I could make it smaller and smaller, but it wouldn't go away, this little black hole of a grave. A drink might help. Driving to the bar, I decided Kenny was a hallucination and the only way to bury him again was to have a drink.

The bartender was right. It was a nice bar full of old ghosts and better times, but still warm and cheery against the blizzard that was gathering its dark forces outside. Buffalo's golden past had found a safe hiding place here. Unemployed workers could drink here all day and tell you about how Buffalo used to be the biggest fresh-water port, the biggest electricity giant. Yes sir, the Industrial Revolution was born here and brought to its knees here, but the lords of the Bull's Head Bar still reigned. Did you know that in the Great War we didn't take rations? And after the war we didn't have a depression. We didn't have to recover with the

New York State Government tax. Shit, we didn't even have prohibition. We could go to Canada and drink. But now the bosses are gone and the mansions are dark. They've taken their business elsewhere. Now they call us the rust belt. Now we don't boast anymore, we just drink. I ordered a shot of Jack Daniels and a Rolling Rock beer.

"We don't have Rolling Rock."

"That's okay. I just like the name. Give me a Bud."

Behind the bar the bartender was much more at ease. He talked about what a crazy guy my dad was and I found it soothing. "It was right in this bar that your dad cut off his finger. I was there."

"You mean he really did that?" In the back of my mind I could see my father's desperate blue eyes. "I guess I always suspected that story about his saving someone at the plant wasn't true."

"Yes, some guy dared him in a bet. We all told him not to. He said okay. Then the next minute he was going to do it again, and we'd have to talk him out of it. It went on all night till we finally didn't believe he would ever do it, and that's when it happened."

I remember Kenny telling me that story like a snake hissing in my ear. I wished he had made it up just to get back at Dad, but even then, I suspected it was true. Little by little the snake removed every shred of respect I had for my father and replaced it with a poisonous pity. I still forgave him because he wasn't trying to convince me my father was a coward; he was trying to convince himself.

"I guess he had to do it just to show us he wasn't a coward." I looked up and the bartender's voice softened, "Well, you know what happened to him in the Army, but he was an awful nice guy." The bartender looked at me for a nod or a word, but I just stared back at him.

Finally, I said, "You mean that his job was interrogating prisoners?"

"No, no, that wasn't how they used him. Ed could never interrogate anyone. He was too nice a guy. Ed was assigned to be an Army witness for interrogations. It was his duty to make sure there was no foul play. Of course, there was nothing but foul play. It was a very nasty war, not like the Second World War. A lot of those soldiers were angry and confused. I mean, Ed knew if he had told what he saw his comrades did, they would have shot him in the back while he was taking a piss. So you see, he had to watch and do nothing while they electrocuted panicked prisoners on their nuts, beat them senseless in the head, did unspeakable things to the girls . . . day in and day out he watched that and said nothing. That does something to a man."

"He was a good man?" I tried not to make it sound like a question, tried not to remember how I turned my back on my dad without any explanation.

"One of the best. Just a little fucked-up in the head, but aren't we all. You better go home or you'll have to spend the night here. It's really coming down."

How come strange bartenders know the truth about your family, while everyone else wonders how such a nice guy can get into so many fights? Why he wants to get beaten up or get his finger cut off. Why he accepts the fact that his daughter doesn't want to talk to him anymore, and he should live in the back room like an animal only coming out at dinner time to howl at the pain he can't reach. I felt dizzy. I walked out into the snow and forgot to pay for the drinks. Outside there was no sound, no wind, just snow everywhere. It was beautiful.

In the car I thought I was in a space capsule landing on another planet. Control was a very if-y subject. The snow kept falling at an alarming rate. Tons and tons of it, where was it all coming from? If I didn't get home I could get stuck on the road. The sky was dark, either from the falling night or storm clouds. I didn't know which. I couldn't remember how long I was in the bar. All I knew was that the road was empty and it kept on disappearing. People do freeze in their cars; they drive off the road and it snows so much their car gets covered, and pretty soon the battery doesn't work and the door won't open – I'm really fucking with my head. Now, stop it. Where the fuck is the . . . road . . .

Far away in the dusk I see it, a little blinking red light. It's the snow plough whose hopeless task is to sweep the snow off the road. I drive towards it not knowing if I'm on the road or not, praying that I won't drive into a ditch. As I get nearer, I can hear the familiar scraping sound, a sound that everyone in this neck of the woods knows. I'm very drunk, but it's okay. As I nestle in behind the snow plough, I am thankful. It's going very slow but I don't care. I'm safe. If it wasn't for the snow plough I would have been lost. Finally I recognize my street and pull away, saying good night to the big machine as it continues all alone on the road, working steadily at its task. As soon as we separate, it disappears in the falling snow. I am alone. Tomorrow morning will be the first time no one shovels the walk to our house. My father is gone.

13

The Indian

As I PULL into our street, the snow is madly trying to bury three brand-new pick-up trucks in front of our house. Indians. Ma's casino friends must have come home with her. If Dad had been alive they would never have gotten in the house. No one thought much of the Indians around here, not even other Indians. They were called the Tuscarora, a wimpy tribe who had been run out of the Carolinas by the Cherokee and came all the way here to join the powerful Northern tribes so they wouldn't get totally wiped out. They were mostly farmers and crafty traders instead of warriors, and to this day you could still get gas and cigarettes at a bargain on their reservation. Now, they owned casinos and drove the latest thing in pick-up trucks. I noticed a woman sitting in one of the trucks. How Indian, I thought, to make your squaw wait in a freezing cold truck. The woman got out and came over to my car. It was a girl about my age. When I got out of my car she looked at me hopelessly.

"Do you want to come inside?"

"No."

We waited, staring at each other.

"Did Bobby come home with you?"

"No, he's in LA, working."

She gave me a funny smile and getting back in her truck she drove off. I was confused. She couldn't have been waiting for me. I don't even know her. She wasn't from our school.

I opened the gate and walked up the drive to our house, the house with the dark room where my mother slept away the day. Kenny and I would wait for the brass knob on her door to turn as the red sun surrendered the sky, signaling that it was okay for us to yell as much as we wanted to up and down the hallway. Even before Kenny, when I was very young, that room was the cave where my mother slept. I remember checking it at least twice a day to make sure she was still there. If I was very still I could hear her breathing in there, then everything was all right. Oddly enough I realized I had a similar cave inside of me. She was in there breathing. Only now, I didn't want her there. I was an adult, a young woman with my own husband and home. It was time for her to leave, but I didn't know how to kick her out.

The house was not empty, as I had wished it to be. My mother sat stiffly on the sofa with her mouth drawn in a stubborn line. I knew that look. No one could change her mind when she looked like that. Next to her with his hand on her arm sat the tall Indian I saw beside her at the funeral. His long black hair looked like a horse's mane but otherwise he was well dressed, as opposed to the other two Indians with greasy black braids who sat across the room pretending not to be there. The Indian next to my mother had been talking to her in a low passionate voice that sounded like water running over rocks, but when I entered, he jumped to his feet like a cat. Extending his hand, he called me by my real name, which only my family used.

"Mei Li," his smile was so friendly I had to stop myself from liking him, "your mother insists on moving to Florida and nothing I can say will stop her."

"She does?" This was the first I'd heard of it. I felt the landscape of my face darken involuntarily. My mother in Florida? To do what? Party on a tropical beach now that my dad was dead?

"Yes, for the weather," answered my mother. "I've never liked the cold. I want to be warm again."

I smiled grimly. This was so typical of my mother, to immediately give you an excuse. She was so secretive, always hiding things in containers, her money in drawers, her past in boxes. It could still sneak up on me, my childhood fear that her heart looked like a giant red chest with lots of little carved doors, and all the feeling in one compartment must never know what the feelings in the other compartments were doing. And if that was true, what if she was to mislay her feelings for me? What if she forgot behind which door she left them and they stayed like a lost pair of gloves in their dark coffin never to be worn by my mother again, never to see the light of day?

"Molly, this is Falling Water."

Immediately I hate this man — standing in my father's house with his hand on my mother's arm. Let's face it, I hate Indians, something I picked up from my dad.

My mother continues in her most formal tone, "He owns the casino up river. You probably don't remember, but you met him when you were very young."

I say nothing. What is there to say? Why is Falling Water smiling at me? Because he remembers me? I don't remember him. Is that why he's looking at me like some strange parent, making me uncomfortable, because I don't have a father anymore? It's something I can't help. I don't want to be without a father. I want this complete stranger to hug me just once before I have to realize that my daddy isn't ever coming back into this house with a smile on his face because he found someone's purse after he had combed the river all day looking for what? What was he looking for? I was cracking up – I could tell the way Ma was staring at me and didn't know what to do.

I stood there as Falling Water explained that he was just leaving, which caused the other two Indians to rise and mumble, backing away from me out the door. I was sure I was going to fall down or make a fool of myself, when the tall man with the long black hair put his arms around me, and pulled me to his chest. For a moment the Christmas lights and sounds of the casino blurred happily around me and I could smell the hint of trees in the wet forest. It was only for a moment, but I never thought I would feel that way again and I started to cry. I wasn't like Ma. I couldn't do everything in private.

After I said good-bye to Falling Water and walked him to the door, he and the other two Indians disappeared quickly into the snow. Snow has a habit of erasing things, one minute it's there and the next minute there's nothing at all. I shut the door.

Alone with my mother I feel empty again. I start

drinking. I want some kind of closure from her but all she does is sit there like a stone. I want her to take me in her arms and cry and tell me she really loved my dad, but that's stupid. Instead I decide to tell her about the man at the funeral who looked like my brother. I don't consider that she might not want to hear it. I want to share it with her. Okay, so I'm drunk. I want to share something with her. I want her to hold me.

Ma doesn't move while I tell her about seeing Kenny. She remains on the couch, while the snow falls heavily again on the other side of the storm windows. It puts a blanket over everything including me. I keep talking but all the excitement I felt is smothered as if my voice is being buried alive. Ma's eyes are cold, like two lumps of coal. Soon all my words dry up and I'm left staring at her, waiting for her to speak.

"You saw a ghost."

"No. It was just some guy."

"Before your father died, he told me he saw Kenny. He spoke to him."

"You think it's true? What did Dad say?"

"Nothing. He was relieved to have a reason for never finding his body. After you left he never stopped looking for Kenny's body. He didn't say he was looking but I knew he was . . . every day.

"Ma, Kenny's not dead? He's alive?" Again that double feeling of anger and joy hit me.

"No. You saw the angel of death. Your father was not sick, but he died the day after he said he spoke to Kenny."

"Ma, this isn't a ghost. What if it really is Kenny? Don't you see? He just pretended to die. The barrel was empty all the time."

Ma looked at me and laughed. It was a threatening laugh, more like a bark telling me to back down. "Why would he pretend to die? You are stupid."

"There are a lot of reasons. One, to show Dad he wasn't a coward like he was always telling him he was."

"Your father never called him that."

"Yes, he did, Ma, all the time."

"You're not making any sense. To show your father he wasn't a coward he would have to stay in the barrel. What you're saying is a cheap joke."

"Ma, all this time I blamed myself. I thought he committed suicide because of me."

May's voice suddenly dropped an octave, "What are you saying?"

"I'm saying that it was the only way Kenny could leave me, by pretending he was dead."

"Why couldn't he leave you?"

There was a silence before May started in a flat emotionless voice, "You think it was because of you he stayed? That you stopped him from going to Harvard? You think you are the reason for everything? You're wrong."

"We were lovers." I desperately thought this truth would finally compel Ma to fold me in her arms and tell me it was all right, but one look at her face told me I was dead wrong.

"What did he do to you?"

"Nothing, Ma. Nothing I didn't want him to do."

"What are you? What kind of whore are you?"

"It wasn't like that. Can't you understand that I loved him? I still love him."

"Shut your mouth, whore."

"Don't pull the big moral act with me. You're the

prostitute in this family. But no one can say anything about that because it's such a big fat fucking secret. Well, everyone knows, so fuck yourself."

"No, you don't know this. Because of me, I make sure you never have to know this."

"Bullshit, I know everything. My dad was the customer who saved your ass and you tortured him."

"I make sure you're not still in China."

"You made him miserable. You made him live in the back room like an animal."

I was not prepared for what happened next. My five-foot-three mother flung herself at me like a large cat with sharp claws flailing. Shocked, I pushed her back against the wall, trying not to hurt her, but she fell. Regaining her feet, she clutched the table, screaming at the top of her lungs in Chinese. Then picking up whatever was on the table, she threw it at me until I managed to run up to her and hit her in the mouth. Blood trickled down May's cut lip. She didn't bother to wipe it away. When she raised her eyes they were dry and dead.

I was scared. "Ma, please stop, stop. Let me . . ."

"No, I'm fine," she seemed a different person smiling crookedly to herself. "I've had a lot worse in my day." Even her voice was different. It wasn't the voice of my mother. The person next to me was very familiar, yet it was someone I did not know. May sat down in the chair with her legs apart and the back of her hand to her mouth. "You're a fool," she said in a quiet matter of fact voice.

"I'm sorry, Ma. I didn't mean to hit you. And I didn't mean what I said." But I did mean it, and there was no way I could take it back. "Ma, I'm proud that you made it all the way here. I've always been proud of you." The words didn't sound proud. They sounded weak.

"You have brought me the last snake's egg, the last humiliation. Go back to your husband. We have nothing more to talk about."

True to her word, Ma stopped talking to me. She no longer stared at me as if everything was my fault, but instead of feeling relieved, I was miserable. She didn't look at me any more than one would look at a chair or the rug. I became a ghost without weight or consequence.

In silence I helped her close the house and pack for Florida. I was amazed how much older she had gotten and how forgetful she was. If she didn't miss my father, she certainly felt lost without him. Was he taking care of her in the end . . . the thought crossed my mind like a shadow. Watching the snow cover everything, I thought the tiny green leaves of spring would no longer fill the branches of our burnt-out oak, and the brown ones would never again whisper their secrets along the ground. The snow was silently covering the trees and bushes with white dust covers like the ones they put over furniture when a house is closed up for vacation. Patiently the furniture waits for the sound of footsteps and familiar voices, but day after empty day, no one returns.

I did not mention Kenny again. Perhaps it was a hallucination. Or maybe what I saw was a death ghost and just that short look into its eyes had already ignited the dormant cancer cells in my body, booby traps I inherited from my mother along with this shark in my guts.

We did not even kiss good-bye. The airport in

Buffalo is nondescript. It's like a gray zone that you must enter before you go somewhere else. It was still snowing outside and everyone had that grim look on their face. Once it snowed for nine days straight. People starved to death because they couldn't get out their front doors. One of the biggest killers in Buffalo, besides car accidents, is heart attacks while shoveling snow. The good thing about Buffalo is everybody is drunk because the west wind off Lake Erie is so cold you can only walk a block before you have to go inside again. People go from bar to bar to get anywhere.

The snow falls quietly as flight after flight is cancelled. The runways are a mess. Some people are lying down on the floor with their heads on their suitcases. This is not a good sign. The happy flight to Florida is not delayed. Everyone watches as these lucky passengers line up to board. They will be frolicking in the Gulf Stream soon while we line the shores of Antarctica, hunched against the freezing winter wind. I am positive that Ma will break down and at least touch me before she boards. As I watch her back walk away from me I am still positive and very wrong.

After putting Ma on a plane, I wander about our house for the last time, listening to Niagara pounding in the distance like a heartbeat under the snow. Slowly, I allow myself to harbor the feeling that Kenny is still alive. The thought sails into my brain and floats in the cove of my skull, a black ship neither landing so that I can believe, nor making me sure of the opposite by leaving. It just stays there as if my brain were under siege. Or is that Kenny's heart beating under the snow?

The same airport again to catch my own plane back to LA. I have the uncanny feeling that someone is watching me. This place is limbo. Nobody belongs here. They're all trying to go somewhere else, either up to heaven or back down to hell. A family of five is noisily eating their Macdonald's poison patties next to me. They will be on the plane to hell because they wouldn't know heaven if they sat on it. Or is that a description of me? I stare at the blonde sitting opposite me just because there is nothing else to look at. She smiles back. In the back of my mind it blooms like the blossom of a black rose underwater, the thought that the man from the graveyard is watching me.

14

House life

⋘❦⋙

WHEN I GOT home, I was so haunted by the bizarre notion that Kenny was still alive, I barely noticed the little canary yellow Volkswagon Bobby had waiting for me. I didn't feel like driving anymore. Escape was futile. Instead I hung around the house all the time in order to be there for another clue, letter, or visit. I became obsessed with the phone. It seemed to me that there were an inordinate amount of wrong number calls. The phone would ring but when I picked it up, the person on the other end would hang up, but not right away. Who would do that but Kenny? It never happened before I saw the man in the cemetery. I convinced myself it was Kenny. After a couple of months of this, I decided to tell Bobby about everything: the man in the graveyard, the phone calls, the feeling that I was being watched. I knew I was running the risk of sounding like I was losing my mind, but so what.

His response was surly and vulgar, "Is that why we're not fucking anymore?"

"What?"

"Because you think he's alive?"

"Bobby, is that all you can think about . . . your dick? I've lost a father and a brother. You don't know what that's like. I need time to . . . to . . . I don't see how you can say that." Later on I thought about it and Bobby was right. Since I had allowed myself to hope that Kenny was alive, everything about Bobby bothered me – hearing him breathing in the next room, or clicking his teeth while we slept. I couldn't sleep with him much less make love with him.

In the back of my mind among the black roses, I was living another life. I was the princess faithfully waiting for the return of her prince. I imagined the country he had gone to, the battles he fought for me. I bought the dress he would see me in when he came back, a scarlet dress, Chinese style. If I had picked a Hollywood movie scenario instead of something out of the fairy tales which my brother and I had spent so much time re-enacting in the woods of Niagara, I would have been less corny and more realistic about Kenny's death, but after all the games we played it was easy for me to cross the flimsy boundaries of reality and think he was only pretending to be dead.

Bobby, on the other hand, never tried to believe Kenny might be alive. Point blank, he called it a hallucination caused by alcohol. Clumsily he started dropping hints about rehab and AA. The more he hinted the stronger and more secretive my other life became, and the more Bobby became the enemy, my scapegoat, my reason to fight instead of being swallowed by grief. There were times when I felt sorry for Bobby. Other times I detested him. I was completely justified. There are things about Bobby no one in their right mind would put up with. For one thing, he was a pack rat. His things were in piles everywhere.

In the beginning, it was just a few things, the clutter of junk we laughingly called stuff. But as more stuff appeared, eating giant amounts of space, it freaked me out. Our house was small. That's when I felt the door shut. It wasn't painted, it didn't have a handle, it wasn't even real, but it was definitely closed and I was acutely aware that my space was limited. The woods of Niagara no longer lay behind me. Here, I was pinned to the cement block on which my little cement house was anchored in the middle of thousands of other cement blocks, and it was all duly celebrated by a lethal little ceremony called marriage. Everything Bobby did seemed to take away another little square of my space.

Out of self-preservation I started erecting boundaries in the house – lines of demarcation – all your stuff has to go over there. If you bring it over here, you have to take it back. But Bobby would forget, and I would spend all my time organizing his junk and marching it across the border. "Okay, you can have the hallway, and some of the living room. The kitchen is ours, but I want the bedroom clear." At this point, I'm screaming like my mom at a volume level far beyond what the situation calls for. What I really want is for Bobby to get out of the house, but he's paying the rent.

In the night I could hear the stuff mobilizing into phalanxes. It moved around the room setting traps for me. It learned how to open doors and move in when I wasn't looking. I would throw something out and the next day it would return, washed-off and better-looking. Bobby, of course, doesn't believe that the army of clutter is seriously advancing on us. He thinks I'm overwrought, high-strung, fucked-up, a bitch, and he's right. I swore I wasn't going to be a ballbreaker like my mom, but here I am taking shots at him whenever I have the least bit of unfair advantage.

Soon we develop a hideous pattern of hatred. At the sound of Bobby's car pulling up to the house, anger erupts in little blisters over my heart. I listen as his car door shuts. Soon the door in the white wall opposite me opens and Bobby enters the room carrying something in a paper bag. "Darling, I've got a present for you," he says in his best let's pretend we're happy voice.

"Bobby, you shouldn't have," I answer, meaning every word. "What is it?" I ask suspiciously.

"A cactus."

"Cactus? I don't like cactus."

"But look at this one, It's planted in a little plastic fat lady and the cactus is growing out of the top of her head like hair."

"You brought that for me?"

"You don't like it?"

An embarrassed giggle jumps from his mouth and skitters across the floor. This is not the same sweet boy who brought me pebbles and glass in the winter and pussy willows in the spring. This is a guy who is guilty because he's not around very much. I suppose he's not around because his wife is a bitch, but I don't care.

"It even looks like you," he continues sheepishly, "but, of course, her tits are too big."

That nervous giggle again. Am I being mocked? I scan Bobby's face for traces of the enemy. Perhaps there is a plot here. Every day it's something new, something I don't like, don't need, and don't want. Is he trying to drive me around the bend? Push me over the edge? That should be easy. I certainly don't have very far to fall. A woman who is waiting for her dead brother to give her a call? Sounds like I've already hit bottom.

The annoying part of the whole charade is he pretends all this stuff is for me, forcing me to say thank you when I really want to say get this shit out of here.

"Get this shit out of here."

"I thought you liked presents."

"Yes, but what I mean is, you shouldn't spend the money."

"It was only three dollars."

"That's just it. One expensive gift, fine, but not a million little pieces of junk. I mean you add all this stuff up and we could have had something nice." My voice slides into the "out of control" register again. I want to hurt him. The shark appears from out of the depths of my psyche, something dark and Asian in my blood – the words echo slightly, but I am too busy yelling to hear them. "But no, you buy crap, crap that nobody wants."

Bobby throws the cactus into the sink, as I continue relentlessly walking back and forth, back and forth, my anger thrashing about like a shark being hauled into a boat.

"It's a sickness. You're the one who is sick. You're addicted to shopping. It's like you're trying to buy the one thing you're lacking – a personality." It was true, without his football uniform he reminded me of a turtle without its shell, unrecognizable, and oddly vulnerable in spite of his size. In an effort to overcome this, he bought things. He bought a hat in the hopes of becoming a person who would own a hat like that. The horrifying thing was the more he bought the more he disappeared, and little by little, over the months I lost him behind the piles of garbage he had dragged home

"I mean, I can't believe you bought skis, yesterday. It's fucking July."

"They were on sale."

"But you have skis."

"These are made of wood. They're antiques."

Even his excuses were boring. Since we were kids, I always pretended Bobby was boring for Kenny's sake, so that Kenny would never feel envious of Bobby's good looks or athletic ability. The truth was, if Kenny was the smartest, Bobby was the more sensitive. Kenny was the brain and Bobby was the body. As kids we labeled things with such determination that now, there is nothing Bobby could bring home that would erase the stigma of boring.

"But, Bobby, you bought two pairs of ski boots."

"In case one fit better than the other, they're second-hand."

"But, damn it, you don't go skiing."

"But I want to."

I don't answer. This is bullshit. Something else is going on, and I don't know what it is.

"Sorry," he says in his bad schoolboy routine.

"Why? Why do you buy this shit – out of guilt?" Out of nowhere, a red flare drops down into my skull. My nerves tighten like soldiers on a battlefield as they watch the flare slide down the night sky. He's cheating on me. That's what's going on.

The thought moves into my bay of possibilities like an iceberg, cold and monstrous. It would be easy for Bobby to fuck around on me.

No, I cross cheating off the list. The one thing I'm

sure of is that Bobby loves me. My whole class knew he was in love with me. He has loved me from the first day I talked to him, when he was fat Bobby. He was friends with Kenny just so he could see me every day, and stand next to me so close that my hair brushed his face. The weight of my body made him tremble every time I leaned against him in the movies. Even Kenny knew. He was always teasing me about it. Asking if I let Bobby kiss me yet, and what it felt like.

Without Kenny, Niagara's big strong football player seemed lost, and for the first time, I wonder if Bobby missed Kenny as much as I did. He never talks about it. I don't know why I'm so mean to him. I don't want to be. I hate it. I have momitus, a congenital disease that makes you turn into your mom. I treat Bobby the way my mom treated my dad, the one thing I promised myself I would never do.

"There's no dinner," I apologize. "I thought we'd go out."

"Like last night?"

"Last night was take-out. I mean a restaurant."

"I can't. I'm seeing a client tonight. Tomorrow, OK?"

"Whatever." I watch Bobby change his clothes. I am embarrassed to say that he still turns me on even though we have stopped having sex.

"I would invite you, but it will be boring, just a lot of car talk."

"No. I don't feel up to it."

Bobby takes a small brown bottle from one jacket to another.

"What's in the bottle?"

"What bottle?"

"That little brown bottle you just put in your jacket. I found two of them in the bathroom."

"What did you do with them?"

"I was cleaning. I threw them out."

"Damn it, Molly, that's sinus medicine."

"I'm sorry. I didn't know. It didn't have a label on it."

"It's herbal, homeopathic, you know, homemade. The label fell off. Just leave my shit alone."

The unfamiliar coldness in his voice sucks the wind out of my sails. Pulling the depression I call daily existence up to my chin like a child pulling up its blanket, I turn my head to the wall. I'm not the same girl without Niagara to back me up. Stuck here in the concrete waste of San Bernardino with the desert wind screaming over my head I need all the undivided attention I can get. Anything less increases the vast flood of insecurity that my ego motors around on. My poor ego can only afford a paper-thin boat, and the slightest swell can easily swamp it.

The idea of Bobby cheating on me continues to bleep in the back of my mind like a hurricane warning. He's not going to put up with me for much longer. The sky grows a threatening bluish black ahead of me, squall winds tilt the sea at a forty-five-degree-angle until the door slams and Bobby is gone. I am alone in the quiet eye of the storm. I hate being alone.

I try to hang on to things but they melt and slip through my brain like silver fish sliding under the blue water. In high school, I had been so sure of myself, so in control. I had a brother and a boyfriend, both in love with me. Now, four years later, I had exchanged my beautiful king and knight for an ugly rook called home life, a house full of shit, and a husband who ignores me.

I have done such a good fucking job of harping on Bobby's defects that I can't imagine us getting back together. Perhaps if I give up the stupid idea of Kenny's being alive, but the phone rings and stubborn hope blossoms like the spring flowers after a crushing winter snow.

"Hello?"

"Mei Li?"

"Yes . . ."

"You must come to Florida. I am dying."

"Ma? Ma, you've only been there a couple of—"

She hangs up on me.

15

Mother's tale

THE "FASTEN SEATBELT" sign came on, a sign that we were leaving the pleasant limbo of white clouds and dropping down into the state of Florida. As I fastened my seatbelt I tried to think of my mother sinking back into the exotic past she had managed to escape from, a small yellow woman living in a thatched communal hut near a Buddhist center, perhaps not even speaking English anymore. Old and unable to endure the Niagara winters, she had slid back into the jungle, the jungle of a disconnected mind and arthritic decaying limbs. She had had me when she was well into her forties and now in her seventies, perhaps she wasn't the same manipulative woman. Perhaps she had mellowed. But I hadn't. Thinking of her, the word "witch" got trapped in my head. As we fell out of the sky, it seemed to pick up speed, bouncing higher and higher off the curved walls of my skull.

Arriving in Tampa I went through the terminal, picked up my baggage, and passed unhindered through the sliding glass doors that admitted one into the terrarium atmosphere Florida is famous for. The humidity and heat dropped on me like a wet blanket trying to follow me into the taxi. Under the punishing tropical climate, something happened to my guts. I seemed to unwind, stretch out, and relax. Perhaps I was part lizard and didn't know it until now. That would explain the problem I was having back home. I knew the system, had been given the rules, and yet I had been unable to adapt. Lizards don't adapt well. Their brains aren't large enough. From now on I had to concentrate. However, concentrating without air conditioning was impossible.

When I got out of the taxi the air tried to smother me again. Palm trees clattered high above my head like shaman rattles, and the ground was white with the sacrifice of crushed sea shells. If reincarnation were true, what if I came back to this planet a small frightened piece of muscle, so frightened all I could do was hide away in my lovely white shell? And the only consolation I had was that there were thousands like me. How terrible to find out that the purpose of my life and the life of all my kind was to pave this hideous driveway.

The ocean must be nearby, tossing on its bed of sand and dreaming of the hurricane women Denise, Edith, Fanny. Down the road I saw a bridge with three people seated on boxes, holding fishing poles. Apparently the air had paralyzed them, or they had forgotten how to move. No one else was around. It was deathly quiet, making me feel slightly disoriented as if I was on another planet whose gravitational pull was twice the strength of earth.

Turning to face a very clean turquoise and white one-story apartment complex, I was puzzled to find that Ma's door had quite a large gathering of pots that were filled with all kinds of overly healthy and heavily pampered plants. Every Mother's Day my brother and I had given Ma a plant, usually a geranium, and for the next three months the household was forced to watch the plant's slow murder at the hands of Ma. I remembered the spindly geranium stalks with only a few pathetically small leaves and at the very end the desperate red flower, the plant's last flare for help before going under. Judging by these new plants, the geranium deaths apparently were the fault of the Buffalo weather, not Ma's lacquer-red nails.

When the door opened I got my second and far more devastating shock. The little old woman on the other side of the threshold was unrecognizable except for her eyes, which held a familiar disapproval. Otherwise her black hair was gray, she wore no make-up on her wrinkled face, and if anything she had gotten shorter. It wasn't until she opened her mouth that I realized all of her teeth were missing, which further explained why she was so different-looking. Reading my face like a mirror, she put her hand in front of her mouth.

"Ma?"

"Good. You're still very beautiful," she said it as if commenting on a clay pot she had made twenty-five years ago.

Putting my arms around the old woman was like holding a bunch of twigs. I thought she would snap and break apart, but instead it was my voice that disintegrated, "Ma . . ."

"Inside. Don't let people see you cry. Get in here." The old woman dragged me inside, slamming the door shut. Immediately the strong smell of urine and rotting food overpowered me. The place was a dark maze of piled-up papers and things. For some unknown reason there were newspapers all over the floor in an irregular pattern, and large note-papers tacked all over the walls, windows, and mirrors. On the notes were scribbled words like "pills," "water plants," "milk," "telephone," "Tuesday." Moths flew out of the carpet and ants crawled along the windowsill. In the garbage were dirty plates and silverware, thrown out instead of washed. The garbage was immense. It filled the little kitchen and threatened the living room. I had stepped into the last stages of a brain trying to function on its own and losing the battle. Either Dad had been taking care of her in his last days or whatever was eating her brain was doing it at an alarming rate.

Ma tried to act as if she were the same and I went along with it, but she put on a very thin show. She scurried around the tiny apartment like a small nesting rodent telling me where to sit, what she had for me to eat, and when she finally got down to criticizing my dress and hair I tried to act like I felt right at home.

"Ma, you're not dying. Why did you say you were?"

"Going to die."

"Did the doctor tell you that?"

"Not doctor, I go to acupuncturist."

"Oh great, they aren't very good with dental hygiene." The conversation stopped. I forgot she must be painfully embarrassed about her missing teeth. "It's all right, Ma. Did the acupuncturist say you were dying?"

"No."

"Well, then, I don't understand."

"I saw the ghost, your brother."

"You saw Kenny, so you think you're dying?"

"I have money left from gambling. If you don't need it I give it to the temple."

For a moment I allow myself to hope she did see Kenny. My heart climbs up my throat as I casually say, "Ma, did Kenny say where he was staying?"

"He's dead, Mei Li. He is death angel. That's why I called you."

"Ma, please, you're not going to die. And Kenny might be a lot of things but angel isn't one of them."

"Not real. An omen," May slams her hand down on the table. "You have not changed. You do not listen, and you make me yell." I shut up. The idea that her yelling all those years was my fault for not listening and not the fault of her alcohol completely stunned me. "I wanted to see you. I am not afraid of dying, I am afraid you will die without past, and I am responsible."

"Ma, what are you saying?"

"Your history, my past, I wanted you to be American so I never told you of your grandmothers and great-grandmothers, and now it is too late."

"It's not too late, Ma. Can we go outside? It's too hot in here."

I didn't know what else to say. The smell is getting to me. Putting on a sweater and sunglasses as big as a car windshield, she finally grabs my arm and lets me take her outside, probably for the first time in months. We sit on the front porch, or what should have been the front porch, but looks more like a driveway, and I am amazed that I can't shut my mother up. "Your name is Mei Li. Your family name is Li, and your name is written in the temple. Mei means beautiful. Li is a very rich and important house in China. My grandmother was the third wife in that house." This little old woman who used to be my mother is so upset over history, something my mother would never talk about, she's shaking as she speaks.

"When my mother was born, girls were unwelcome, so they took her to the Master's mother, your great-great-grandmother, expecting she would not save the child. She was powerful woman always dressing in long green sleeves that touch the ground, blind eyes that were luminous as the inside of a shell, teeth stained blood-red from beetle juice, and hair white as foam. Everyone was afraid of her. To everyone surprise she let my mother live, saying the lowly girl child was the only future of great house of Li. She was right. She and her entire house slaughtered by the Japanese in the Rape of Nanking. Many Chinese killed by the Japanese. Everything destroyed. You don't understand how that can happen, but when it does you do anything to survive. My mother survived pregnant with me, but dead in childbirth. With me all hopes of the old woman in green sleeves survive. I am the wind that brought you here and planted you, but now, up to the plant to grow its own roots."

"Are you trying to tell me you want a grandchild?" I smiled, not really able to keep track of her story and wanting to get to the point.

"LISTEN TO ME," Ma screams. Her knuckles hit the chair with such force I looked for blood. "Generations, the house of Li, the old woman, your great-grandmothers, what I have done, all will be nothing. You owe them. You owe me."

She was either trying to guilt-trip me or she was

losing it. I remember my mother insisting she had no past. She vaguely remembered her mother being a peasant woman. Either she was making this story up or illusion was the final stage of old age. Perhaps all old people, having no future, look to the past and it makes them go mad. I began to feel sorry for her. "What, Ma, tell me what you want."

"You cannot drift . . . have no roots, no grand-mothers, no ancestors. Without roots the tree is destined to become worthless driftwood."

"Don't be silly, Ma. I have a marriage, a house, a car."

"These are possessions, not roots."

I was beginning to understand. What she was saying was all projection. It was Ma whose roots were rotting, whose strands of memory were loosening their grip on the earth, on all the things she had known, and she was drifting out into a black void. I couldn't swim out there, grab hold of her, and pull her back. No one could help her.

"Like twig in the river you float, bouncing off rocks and stones. You don't know to hold on . . . my fault. I did not teach you. I try, give you artificial American roots but they are worthless pieces of junk." She hits her chair again in a rage that's alarming.

If she was trying to insult me or terrify me, it was beginning to work. I didn't like what she was saying, and I wanted to change the subject, "Okay, then tell me about the past, about Vietnam."

May got up and went into the house. When she returned she was holding a photograph which she handed me rather sheepishly. Still, I was not prepared for what I saw. The man was not my father. He was a soldier-of-fortune-looking guy, a combination of good looks and violence, and with him was an incredible Asian sex bomb that had nothing to do with my mother. The last old photo I saw of my mother was a bride in a fancy wedding dress looking rather stiff and not all that sexy. Well, not as outrageous as the creature in this shot – she was completely intimidating and at the same time intensely compelling in a very basic animal way. All of which made me feel at once drab and unglamorous. I stared at the photo not knowing what to say to her. She grinned like a little kid.

"I was always going to show you this, but I was always so embarrassed."

"You don't have anything to be embarrassed about . . . you should have been a movie star. Who is the guy?"

"Bad, very bad. Killed many men." She said it softly as if she were boasting to her girlfriends. Staring at the photo, my mind started running on like a cheap romance novel. This was my father, a real soldier, a fighter, not the sad man who shoveled our walk in the early morning snow, the drunk who was so painful to love. And if this was my real father, Kenny and I were not related. We could even be married. "Ma, are you trying to tell me something about this man?" I asked hopefully.

Her eyes bore into me like two drill bits. "No." Knowing exactly what I meant, she snatched back the photo.

As a peace offering I reached into my purse and pulled out a smart-looking box. "I have something for you, too. Here, open it." May attacked the box with the intensity of a small rodent after its dinner. Pulling a small jade pendant out of its wrapper, she held it up to her withered neck, and her face melted into a rare smile of pure pleasure. I got up and helped her put it on. For a fraction of a second she is beautiful and I am a small girl helping her dress again. Holding up little jade earrings May whispered happily, "Very beautiful. I will wear them to bed."

"Ma, it's only three o'clock, you can't be tired. Let's get something to eat?"

"No, I go to bed now. You check into the motel around the corner. Kiss me."

"Do you want me to help you put on the earrings?"

"No, I want something to hold on to. Thank you." I had to walk her to her bedroom where she lay down, instantly becoming part of the garbage. The sheets were gray with dirt and the room again was filled with newspapers. I was exhausted and nervous. This was my mother, Dr Ming, the woman I hated, but instead of leaving her on her pile of garbage, I was already making a shopping list of items I would need to clean the place. Shit, what if she didn't have a washing machine? Maybe I should just buy new sheets, new carpets. Oh God, I was having decorating problems and I hadn't even bought a can of Comet yet.

I started picking up a few things, thinking I should hire professionals to do this, when a coffee can slipped through my fingers. The lid flew off and gold kruger-rands spilled out. Forget the professional cleaners.

"Ma, do you have money hidden in this house?"

"What?"

"Money, Ma? Did you hide it in here?"

"I don't remember where." These were her last words to me. They sounded so weak that I panicked. Where was Dr Ming? Where was the Dragon Lady? Gone, and in their haste they left me with this little old child. I didn't know what to do. I started cleaning as if that would bring her back. I went into the kitchen where the garbage was overflowing in bags. Tipping one over, I fished out a set of false teeth, which were under a bundle wrapped in newspaper and string. There was ten grand inside the newspaper. Needless to say I started cleaning very carefully, checking everything.

It was as if the apartment was the inside of her brain and restoring it to its proper functioning level would jump-start Ma's ability to function. Every plate, every spoon had to be in its proper place so that when the sun went down Ma would get up, put on her new jade earrings, and be herself again. But she didn't get up. The moon floated across the black waters of the sky until it sank out of sight, turning the sky an ugly steamy yellow.

I had worked all night and all I had was a suitcase full of cash, a fairly clean apartment, and a much bigger problem. Ma did not get up again, and she did not speak another word except in Chinese, nor would she eat except to take water. She wasn't sick. I called everywhere until I found a Buddhist temple. They knew her and sent a monk over to see to her, while I went back to my motel exhausted. If she died I was afraid I would start drifting like she described.

Lying on the queen-sized bed of my motel room, I was haunted by the photo of my mother as a young sexy girl. Her eyes stared straight ahead, daring me to look at her half-naked body. I went over my earliest recollections of Ma, searching for traces of that girl. I wanted to see that girl again, but sleep overtook me.

The casino filled my brain. I loved the casino. It was

like being inside a big clock where things spun around making ringing and ticking noises. Ma walked through the crowd like a miniature Egyptian queen gliding down the Nile, while I was carried behind her by Falling Water. His long black hair moved behind him as his strong arms held me all the way to the car as tenderly as if I was his own child. In the car I watched him through the window kissing my mother good night. As he bent down towards her face, I saw the girl in Ma's photo smiling up at him. I watched her red nails run through his hair and her red mouth devour his lips. And I heard her laugh. She never laughed at home like that and I remember thinking she's like me. She likes to go inside the clock.

16

Ghost

I WOKE UP in the strange motel room because the phone was ringing. "Hello?"

Ma's voice was on the other end, small and far away. "I saw him."

"Who?"

"Kenny, your brother, I saw him again."

"Does that mean you'll eat something?"

"He told me not to tell you he was here. He also said he loved you."

"I know, Ma."

"He has dyed his hair."

"Ghosts don't dye their hair.

"His hair is blond."

"Ma? Tell me you're not lying. You know, seeing things."

"Don't be stupid. I know what I saw."

"He's not a ghost? He's really Kenny?"

"He's a ghost."

"Are you sure?"

"He was standing right here."

"Where is he now?"

"He told me not to tell you."

"Did he say where he was staying?"

"No, he comes out of the clouds at night."

"Ma, listen to me. Where did he say . . ."

The phone clicked off. I had fallen asleep in my clothes, so it couldn't have taken me any more than five minutes to get to my mother's apartment, but still I was too late. Ma was dead. She died of natural causes, a heart attack is what they said, but I didn't believe them. For one thing the necklace and earrings were missing. When I mentioned it, the cops seemed reluctant to say that it was a robbery, and when I told them about her seeing my supposedly dead brother, they said she must have been hallucinating, a very common thing when one is forced to come to terms with death. They offer me a drink. I tell them I don't want one. This is the one time when everyone is supposed to get drunk, they tell me. They set the drink on the table in front of me. They are staring at me, like I was going to be a problem, so I start crying. I can't stop. It comes in waves from an ocean I can't see. They suggest I go back to my motel and get some rest. "We'll be around with papers for you to sign," is what they say.

On the way back to the motel I bought a bottle of vodka, but I didn't open it. I put it on the TV like some sort of decoration. The next thing I knew, I woke up in the same motel room because the phone was ringing.

"Hello."

"Hi, Mei Li."

Dead silence . . . My mother was dead, my father was dead, and my brother was dead. These were the only three people who knew to call me Mei Li. "Who is this?"

"Come on, it hasn't been that long."

"Kenny? Where are you?" There was no answer but I could feel someone smiling on the other end.

"In hell, it's a long-distance call."

"Please, tell me where you are."

"Surf Side Motel, four blocks away."

"I knew it. I knew you were alive. I want to see you."

"You can't, Kenny's dead."

"Kenny, stop it. Stop it. I have to see you."

"Calm down, Scarlet. You cleaned the house. It looks good."

"Kenny, I just had this dream that Ma died."

"She's fine, I just saw her."

I stare at the TV. There is no bottle of vodka on it. It's embarrassing to know you want your mother dead. You want it all to be over, so you dream it is. The final clean-up. Fear seeped up from the base of my skull.

"Don't leave without seeing me." There wasn't any response on the other end. "Did you hear me? Kenny, please." My voice is frantic.

"Okay. There's a Beachcomber Bar next to my motel. Meet me there in fifteen minutes."

I have to move quick before this too becomes a dream. Wearing the same clothes, which were beginning to feel like a second skin, I left the Ocean View Motel and drove to the Beachcomber. I couldn't find my car keys fast enough so I walked. A sister on her way to see her lost brother, a girlfriend on her way to see her lover, another unsuspecting person going to meet her angel of death – I didn't know. I had no reason not to believe that Kenny would take me in his arms and we would escape into the sunset, but something told me it wasn't going to be that simple. The old double emotion started tearing at my throat, hating him for leaving and loving him for returning. At the Beachcomber I was sweaty and out of breath. Instead of walking, I had run four blocks.

Going from the bright Florida outdoors with its quietly dying palm trees in their sidewalk coffins into the dark depths of the bar was like traveling down into a nether world populated by ghosts and lost souls. Here, there was no sunlight. The objects in the bar glowed luridly from thousands of tiny Christmas lights hidden in the underwater decor of starfish, nets, clumps of cork, and sea shells. Here and there a stuffed fish held its mouth open in panic like some Bosch monster trapped in the floating garbage of hell. There were only two people in the bar, a customer and a satanic-looking bartender covered in blue tattoos and the latest in piercing and stapling, which he proudly revealed by wearing only black leather shorts and boots. The customer looked tame in comparison, just your average young alcoholic woman drinking her way through the afternoon. When the bartender said he hadn't seen anyone matching Kenny's description, I decided to join the blonde. She smiled at me and raised her glass. For a moment we were sisters hiding out together.

For a blonde bar fly she wasn't as floozy as I expected. Actually she was dressed better than I was: make-up low key, classy coat and slack outfit, sexy shoes, designer sunglasses, and jade earrings. She picked up her expensive handbag along with the *New York Times Book Review* under it and sauntered over to me. Taking off her sunglasses, she couldn't help grinning at me. Her eyes glittered like pieces of cut green glass, but I held my cool.

"Hello, Kenny."

"I didn't think you'd recognize me."

"I don't. I recognized Mom's necklace and earrings. I just gave them to her."

"Well, they are mine now. She gave them to me." I changed my mind; it was Kenny who looked satanic. As he lit a cigarette, swaying back and forth like a hooded cobra, I didn't know if it was because he was unsteady on his heels or because he was about to strike. "Everything else she's leaving to some temple."

"How do you know that?" I felt like I had been put into an alternate reality or a movie about my life where they got the gender wrong.

"Because I tried to talk her out of it." Kenny took a drag on his cigarette and threw back his head. "What brings you here? I thought you hated her, or do you know about her little nest egg?" Pulling three bankbooks out of his back pocket, he tossed them on the table.

"Where did you get those?"

"From her purse."

"You went through her purse?"

"Yes, I went through her purse before I put her in the hospital. Did you leave her there to starve to death while that crazy monk lit candles and smoked incense?"

"I didn't know what else to do." The silence is unbearable. I'm afraid of him, afraid he'll leave, afraid he hates me. I change the subject. "I liked you better with black hair."

"The dye job is just for the show."

"You act now?"

"A drag show I'm doing." He smirks, "I don't usually dress like this."

"Then, why did you?" My mind is racing. We're in hell. I'm talking to a dead man and I feel nothing. I'm dead myself.

"Because the idea of explaining to you that I'm gay is boring. So I thought I'd just give you a visual image. You know, a picture is worth a thousand words."

"Thanks." I hate this person in front of me. I hate him.

"You know she has quite a nest egg?"

"From gambling. That's why she wants to give it away."

"Well, I need all I can get. I don't have a Bobby looking after me. By the way, how is Robert?"

"Don't you want to know how I'm doing?" I'm alarmed at how my voice sounds, shrill and unstable.

"Yes, yes," he hisses sarcastically, "By all means, let's just talk about you. And lower your voice."

"Yes, me, your sister." I wasn't going to let him get out of it, not if he was a girl, not if he was a talking corpse. I lower my voice. "Your lover. I was in love with you." When the same vacant sad look flashes across Kenny's face, melting his make-up, I finally recognize something and start to cry. It really is Kenny.

"Come on, Sis. Have another drink." Some other people have stumbled into the bar. They are looking at us. They know what's going on, an emotional tear in the social fabric. Soak it in alcohol. Get it numb before the rip spreads and everybody has to start sewing their lives back together.

I down another shot of vodka and try to make sense of what is happening to me. "Look, Kenny, I don't want to talk this way. I don't want to make jokes, and I don't want to blame you. I understand why you ran. The humiliation of incest can do – "

"You don't know the first thing about humiliation." The snake was coiled to strike again. Having never been on the opposite end of one of Kenny's attacks, I held my ground preparing for the worst, but he uncoiled and continued in a softer voice. "Yes, I was in love, crazy with love. The kind of love that makes you do stupid things." With both hands he pushed his hair back from his face and for another second I saw the Kenny I used to know.

"We both did." I put a sympathetic hand on his shoulder, but he pulls away.

"We were not in love. It wasn't you that I was in love with. I was in love . . . with Bobby. I was desperate. And the only way I could get him to hang around was by dangling my little sister in front of him. But I didn't want you two to start fucking and leave me out. So I let you think we were in love. Pretty Machiavellian, right? It was the only way I could keep you two apart. I got to say though, you were born to be a cock-tease. I just switched you on, but when you got going, you were genius."

"Wait a minute. I wasn't a cock-tease. I did it for you."

"Honey, you were the cock-tease from hell."

"What about you? You tell everyone you're dead. Then you come back and tell me you're gay. You might as well be dead. I still can't have you."

"Is that all you can think about? Try growing up and facing reality instead of whining about what you want."

"Reality?"

"Yes, I was always gay."

"But I didn't – "

"Notice anyone but yourself." Now Kenny is too loud. The bartender comes over and Kenny orders two martinis in a voice that reassures him there is not going be a fight.

Kenny continues in a more normal voice, "I know this isn't the best way to tell you, but I'm doing this twelve-step program and you're one of the people I have to apologize to."

"Twelve-step? Kenny, we're sitting in a bar. You just ordered a martini."

"Yeah, my first in two months." Kenny shrugs and smirks. "But this is a stressful situation."

"Are you listening to yourself?"

"Let me finish! Anyway, the only way I could get boys at school was when their girlfriends wouldn't put out. So, it made sense for me to lie to you at the time and I'm sorry."

I close my eyes. The tree house falls down, Niagara freezes and cracks as great pieces fall off. The deserted factories don't have any giants living inside them. I don't know who I am. Kenny's apology drags on but I can't understand what he is saying. There is only one question I am interested in: "Did you and Bobby have sex?" Wild horses could not have ripped me away from hearing the answer. Like an insane masochist I sit there waiting for more details.

"Are you listening to me, Molly? I had sex with everyone. Teenage boys like to get blown, if it's available – no strings attached. Sure I blew Bobby, more than once. But that wasn't enough. I wanted him to love me the way he loved you. I wanted his eyes to follow me around the room the way they followed you. I wanted him to dream about me at night like he told me he dreamt of you, and most of all I wanted him to cry over me."

"Cry?" I couldn't eliminate the contempt in my voice.

"Yes, cry. You were so mean to him, even I was amazed."

"I wasn't mean. I never did anything to him."

"I know, you completely ignored him. It used to break him up."

"But I didn't love him, I loved you."

"Can't lie to me, I was there, remember? You were in love with yourself, baby. You were in your own world. You made the rules, and if we didn't obey we didn't exist. Welcome to the real world, princess."

Anger curled the inside of my stomach like flames burning paper and turning it black. My voice was laced with contempt. "The twelve-step program? What did you do, apologize to Dad and give him a heart attack?" Kenny's righteous act deflates and I see my opening. The skin along my back tightens as if a dorsal fin were pushing out of my backbone. I hit the sides of my tank, swimming in tighter and tighter circles. "Well, I'm not going to roll over and die, you fucking killer. You let me believe a lie, and it's fucked up not only my marriage but my whole life. You knew I didn't know what was going on."

"Okay, Molly, so now you know. Now what?"

"Were you and Bobby laughing at me all this time? I mean, did you enjoy not telling me?"

"No, that's the way Ma wanted it. You were the perfect American girl with the perfect picture life. As for Bobby, he'd never tell you. Guys are afraid of that shit. Besides he loves you so he doesn't want you to know he sucks dick. So don't go home and confront him."

"What are you saying? Are you telling me not to go home and tell my husband he's a cock-sucker?" The entire bar turns to look at the Chinese girl who was stupid enough to marry a cock-sucker.

Kenny starts pushing me towards the door. "This is why I met you in a public place, to avoid a scene."

"Answer me, God damn you, you little faggot."

My skin is twitching. I lunge for Kenny. Within seconds he is a bloody headless carcass bouncing along the floor. But it's my carcass that's rolling on the floor. Somehow I have fallen down as Kenny struggles to get me out the door. Breaking out of the bar like a drowning man breaking the water's surface, my lungs are exploding, my mouth hiccuping and gasping mouthfuls of air as the palm trees rattle merrily, and the sun sparkles on the pavement.

In the street I push him away. He doesn't follow. It's as if he can't live in the sunlight. He's forced to retreat back to the subterranean depths of the bar, back to limbo where ghosts belong. Let him stay there and feed off Ma's suitcase full of money. They both deserve each other. I can escape, escape from taking care of Ma, from a past that has double-crossed me.

On the way to the airport I realize I never saw the ocean. I didn't have to see it. It lay glittering in the back of my mind, an interior ocean. A dark void lapping at the edges of my brain, it surrounded the small island of my soul. Some day my mother will no longer exist. She will join that ocean. And so will I.

17

An affair

〜〜〜

THE RELAY BOARD lights up inanely, "PLEASE WATCH YOUR LANGUAGE." I laugh and, nudging the man next to me, point at the billboard, "Unbelievable. If you asked a Chicago Bears' fan to do that he'd tear your head off."

The man gives me an apprehensive look. "You're in Anaheim California now." He says it almost like a warning.

"I know," I snort. "Behind the orange curtain. And sitting in this stadium watching the Angels play is just as boring as sitting in church. Of course, sitting in church is like sitting in a game show." My audience turns his attention back to the safety of baseball, indicating the end of the conversation, but I don't let that bother me. "I've been to the Crystal Palace here, angels flying around looking more like Vanna White than Gabriel . . . Do you know what they have on the altar? A phone. And do you know who calls on that phone?

God. God is on the other end, and I have to wonder how God likes being there."

The man starts to look around uncomfortably. He is thinking of moving to another seat if he can find one, but even this doesn't stop me. "Let's face it," I continue in a very pleasantly loud voice. "Prayer was bad enough, but a telephone? I mean you gotta wonder how God likes his privacy being invaded? But, hey, that's not really the point, is it? I mean, think about it, God. Wow, we haven't heard from him since the Ten Commandments. So, you know, let's clear this up for once and for all, who do we kill, and who do we love?"

"Would you please hold it down, lady."

"No wait, you gotta hear what God said when they phoned him up . . . And the message is . . . God needs money for his new TV station."

"That's it." The man gets up to go to the rail to watch, but I refuse to be cut off.

"Well, you know what I say?" I call after him. "Big deal. That's right. I need a few things too, like some new air to breathe."

It's a high pop fly, and it's foul. "Fuck you, can't you fucking hit the fucking ball right?" I yell out. Everyone including the man at the rail looks at me. For a paranoid moment the whole stadium is looking. I duck into the ladies' room. I am having an obscenities attack. "Fuck your mother, fuck Kenny, fuck me, fuck yourself, Oh, go get fucked," I bark at myself. Great, I'm sitting in a public bathroom swearing to myself – this is not a good sign. I know what you're thinking, that I'm tipsy, been nipping at the bottle again. Well, you're right. I just happen to think baseball is boring, and I'm flat out fucking drunk.

Leaving the rest room I definitely do not feel like returning to my seat. I feel like another drink, that's what I feel like. While climbing up to the highest bleacher I tell myself it's to get a little perspective on life, you know, to look down on things, and to have a drink from the bottle of vodka I've taken to carrying in my purse. The upper bleachers are empty and I can drink in private. Looking around, I don't feel closer to heaven up here, all the Angels look like insects. I feel confused. I haven't told Bobby about seeing Kenny. I never tell Bobby anything. I don't trust him anymore, not since I came back from Florida.

The nightmare replays itself in my head. The plane was late. After seeing Kenny, I couldn't wait to get home to my own bed, into the safety of my normal middle-class suburban marriage. I had to heal the gaping wound in the side of my ego where Kenny had broadsided me. For the first time I was mortified that we had sex, that I said I loved him and meant it. Now, I dreaded anyone finding out that we were lovers. Thank God we kept our affair a secret. Thank God Bobby didn't know. Thank God good old faithful Bobby still loved me and I could still crawl back into his arms. I would make up for treating his love so casually: I would cook him gourmet meals, pay attention to the office intrigues, and give him the best fuck of his life preceded by a blow job that would erase all traces of Kenny. Damn Kenny, first he leaves me and now he says he never loved me, and his excuse is that he is gay. He's always so fucking blameless. Someday I'll get him back, but now, I have to sew together the quilt of my past in a way that makes me look a little better.

Snuggling down between the sheets I watch Bobby

get undressed. I can't wait to feel the reassuring touch of his hands. All of his actions are slow, graceful and animal. The way he touches things is sexy, with just one finger first and then the rest of his hand. And the way he always stares directly at me when we make love, although I am positive he isn't thinking of anything in particular, is a turn-on. If most of his habits used to annoy me, sex was definitely not one of them. Uncurling my toes and stretching out my legs in anticipation, I feel something weird at the bottom of the bed that makes me jump. Flipping on the overhead light I throw back the covers. There exposed on the white sheet lies a skimpy pair of bright purple thong underpants. I stare at them so long they seem to squirm in an embarrassed effort to get off the bed.

"Whose are these?"

"Honey, I don't know."

"You don't know? They're not mine."

"Did you get someone else's laundry by mistake?"

"Do you think I'm stupid?"

"Oh shit, I forgot. I let Jack use this place this afternoon. He's dating a married woman on the side. She must have left them."

"A married woman who wears purple thong underwear?"

"Yeah, she's a real pill. Just throw them out. We can't return them."

"You throw them out."

"Molly, where are you going?"

"To get clean sheets." And that was it. The doors rolled shut. All of my weapons and ammunition were silently rolled into place. I didn't say anything more about anything. Instinctively, I pretended that I believed his excuse, following my mother's rule never to fight in the open. I was under siege from all sides, first my brother and now my husband. Everyone is my enemy. No one is to be trusted.

Obviously, Bobby's cheating has been going on for some time. I guess I sort of knew and didn't want to admit it. It was easier to drink and pretend there was no war, but now that's impossible. As my miserable ego listened I unrolled the battle plan. First we need to get even, to have our own affair. Then, when he is afraid of losing me, when he's weak, that's when we'll move in. No one is listening, but it's the only plan I can think of and I have to do something.

The baseball game is over. People are crawling out of the stadium like ants doggedly following one another in long pointless lines. Looking down from where I sit gives me the impression that if I stepped on a few people in line the others would simply continue to file over their bodies in relentless insect-like fashion. I try to concentrate on making my way back to my seat where I hope Jack is waiting for me, because remembering my last drunken experience in a car park, I know I would starve to death before I recognized our car. Either that or I would have to wait until everyone else went home before I could make an educated selection, and that could be as late as three in the morning. I know it's an American sin to say this, but to me all cars look alike.

"Molly."

It's Jack.

"Molly, over here."

It pleases me that Jack's skinny cockiness looks a little shaken at the thought of having lost me, or was his pride dented by the idea that I might have left him? Want to know why I'm with Jack? Well, I'm having an affair with him in an effort to keep some of my ego intact while my lying sack of shit husband cheats on me. That's the battle plan so far: to fuck my husband's competition so it really hurts when he finds out.

Jack and Bobby are salesmen in Uncle Morry's car dealership, but that's where the similarity between the two ends. Bobby is big and easy-going while Jack is wiry, nervous and, like all small men, concerned with his size. He is constantly focusing on the size of every-thing from cars to tits. Needless to say it's my height that attracted Jack to me. In Jack's world height is a measure of his conquest, the same way a mountain climber judges his mountain.

Of course, behind all this fascination with size looms fear. None of the brooms or mops in the house Jack grew up in had any handles, because he was constantly cutting off six-inch sections of any wooden handle into which he could stick three-inch nails so that when he wrapped his hand around the wood, the nails would stick through his fingers forming a lethal imitation of brass knuckles. In adult life nothing changed for Jack. Fear made him slightly paranoid, extremely aggressive, and racist. Since paranoia and aggression had been his companions since childhood, any suggestion that they were problems which most people paid a lot of money to be rid of was considered a serious territorial attack.

I mistook Jack's aggressive manner as the sign of a winner, betting Jack would succeed ahead of my easy-going husband, who seemed to have left all his aggression on the football field. Frankly, I doubted if

Bobby would even have a job if it wasn't for his Uncle Morry.

Jack grabbed my arm and expertly propelled me through the ant farm of humans and cars. All of this is not just a battle plan, it's a vacation too. For instance: you don't like the life you are living? Escape into another world by taking a lover. Men can't do this. When they take on a woman she becomes part of their life, but a woman gets to change lives with every man she sleeps with. In fact men are like magic flying carpets; you can visit different lands, become rich or poor without working, become religious by marrying a priest, become a cowboy by having an affair in Texas, join the political game by blowing the President, and tomorrow get high with a pop star. Society is a wonderful thing if you're a woman, you really can go anywhere so long as a man's first priority is to get laid, and that will never change. Men are pussy hounds and frankly, I'm surprised Jack and my husband are selling any cars at all considering the extramarital time they are both putting in.

So, why Jack? Why not a cowboy, or the President, or even the box boy at Ralph's who tried to sell me reefer in the parking lot? Because they didn't ask me. And Jack did. One day, when I went to get a check from Bobby at the dealership – Bobby wasn't there, but Jack was.

After the baseball game I really wanted to get another drink, but Jack would have gotten angry so I didn't mention it. Once inside the more intimate cocoon of our car I made an effort not to appear too drunk. Jack no sooner locked onto the steering wheel than he became obsessed with traffic, car position, and whose turn it was to go. I could have been in a coma, and it wouldn't have mattered. I'm not whining, far from it, I find it comforting. I like being left alone. In a strange way Jack and I are very well suited for each other. He's so rude, I'm never in any danger of feeling obligated; on the contrary, I feel quite free and independent with him. These are the things you tell yourself when you are fucking your husband's competition in the car deal-ership. You never say, I was fucking Jack because I couldn't get anything better. Looking at Jack I try to remember why I like him.

Half Jewish, half Italian, Jack's explosive dark looks had been good enough to make him come all the way from Brooklyn to seek a movie career. However, his talent only got him as far as car sales. Still, this didn't stop him from sitting in bars and talking as if he were on intimate terms with the Mafia, as if his life was a movie with Robert de Niro. It was exciting for about five minutes until you realized that the stories were repeating, and they were going to continue repeating indefinitely. Jack liked to hear himself talk.

By the time we reach Jack's house I'm almost sober and cranky, which would have upset Bobby but, like I say, Jack doesn't notice. He pulls off my clothes while pushing me in the direction of the bed. The room is clammy and dark. His tongue searches for my tongue, and I can feel his saliva leak into my mouth as he lowers himself down on me to make love. His saliva is much cooler than mine, and it enters my territory as silently as a snake, setting off the poison alarm in my brain. We have been caught by the enemy. It's a trap. They hold us down and they begin to torture us. My body watches helplessly as the intravenous drip of venom continues. The insidious trickle of saliva is a new form of chemical death. Immediately I tell Jack we can't kiss while fucking – it ruins my concentration. He is not bothered at all by my request. He continues. His method of making love is to keep on pumping till he comes. I help him just to get it over with. Not at all like what I'm used to, the slow rhythm that Bobby was capable of. My great battle plan to have an affair to get back at Bobby has backfired. Jack's bed has turned into a humiliating defeat for my army. Across the sheets lie the heroic pieces of my ego in twisted positions that can only mean one thing, that they will never get up again. I have to leave them here. No one must know.

Through the slats in the blinds, chunks of legs and bathing suits can be seen. The sounds of families barbecuing and drinking beer around the tiny swimming pool slide in and out of the room while we continue to make love.

"Both of you, get out of the pool if you're going to do that."

"You're so wet. You want me, Molly? Tell me you want me."

"Don't push her head under the water like that."

"Yes, I want you."

"No, I hate hot dogs."

"Oh God, Molly, that feels so good."

"Please, can I go swimming now?"

"No, first you have to eat."

If the sounds had been in a foreign language it would have been erotic to have them just a venetian blind away while he plays with my cunt, but good old American words make me feel pornographic. His hands are worse than unbearable, they are annoying. To get through this I concentrate on composing a letter home. Dear Dad, I have been caught by the enemy and am being tortured. Like you said, war is hell. I'm happy you're not here, Molly.

Jack lives in one of those U-shaped two-story apartment buildings that have a tiny swimming pool in the courtyard. Puddle might be a more appropriate word because it is too small to swim a lap in. Los Angeles is littered with these useless aqua blue squares; you can see them glinting in the smog as your plane descends into the Los Angeles airport like pieces of smashed blue glass in the dirt. Jack wants me to take a swim after we make love, probably to show me off to the tenants, but I feel like a shark in an aquarium.

I saw a live shark in the desert of all places, at the Pomona State Fair. The sign on the giant blue semi-truck read, LIVE SHARK SHOW, and when the sides were lifted up the glass wall underneath revealed that the inside of the truck was indeed an aquarium with three very live sharks a good two to three feet larger than myself. With nothing but a pair of cut-offs and a plastic air hose the truck driver swam among the sharks, even caressed them. Talking to him later, I found out that he wasn't insane, he was Australian. And no, he didn't think they liked him, but they accepted him. He reassured me, they always gave off warning signs before attacking. Digesting this new information I suddenly became concerned for the obviously fair-minded sharks. The Australian boy answered my questions without the least bit of feeling for his fishy partners.

"These ones here are nearly worn out. They only last three months in captivity."

At once my skin tightened in the desert air as if it had already been nailed to a taxidermy board, and my hands reached for the sides of my throat where my gills had closed over. In the little aquarium of my affair how long will I last, circling and circling until my dorsal fin drops off and I finally lie on the bottom of the tank?

Terrified, I refuse to be displayed in Jack's pool. Of course, Jack once again is completely unsympathetic, and since he has to show something off he puts on all three thousand dollars of his scuba equipment and goes out to sit on the bottom of his pool for twenty minutes. Lying on the bed and knowing he is out there impersonating a human fish in his tank, I try to cheer myself up. After all, not many women have a human fish for a lover, a tame fish that walks to his own tank all dressed up in rubber. I'm sure to be the envy of some women.

When Jack returns from trying out his scuba equipment in only seven feet of chlorinated water he says he had a great time, like I missed out on something. Rather than tell him he's wrong, I close my eyes. The truth is, no amount of imagination, or flying carpet theory, is going to glamorize this sordid little affair. There are times when Jack's world is so small nobody could fit into it, not even this amazing shrinking woman. But then Jack has other valuable qualities, like his incredible frankness.

"You know, fucking you is the only thing that makes up for the fact that Bobby got that promotion."

"Bobby got a promotion?" I was shocked.

"I just found out. It's because his uncle owns the place. But I don't care. I may be working for the guy, but I'm still fucking his wife."

"And is Bobby fucking that lady in the front office?"

"Bobby fucking Michelle? Listen, your husband has better fish to fry, and believe me, she's tried. I've been there. She's a hard person to say no to."

"You fucked her?"

"Of course I fucked her. You want me to lose my job?"

"Right. Of course." Michelle just sounds like another stranger trying to escape from her tiny island of marriage by way of magic carpet. I wasn't angry with her. And Jack? Who could be angry with Jack? If it weren't for Jack's crass frankness I wouldn't have the proof that any of this was going on. So, why am I angry?

"Jack, does your wife own purple underwear?"

"Yeah, how did you know that? I bought them for her on Valentine's Day. You know, a kind of peace offering. I guess it worked because she's not mad at me anymore."

"Jack, will you call me a cab?"

"Why? You got to go to the hospital?"

"No, I'm going home. Our affair is over." What else was I going to do? Tell him, I know you're trying to poison me with undetectable snake saliva? He might think I was going mad . . . now there's a thought . . . I let it sink inside my head like a stone into a pail of mud.

Announcing that I'll call my own cab, I march out of Jack's place. The trouble with LA is the nearest phone could be anywhere from half a block to half a mile away. The remaining troops of my army are demoralized and tired. They want to go home and sleep forever. They are ragged and they don't march in formation anymore. I left my make-up at Jack's, not to mention my wallet and all my money. While walking, I try to boost morale by revealing plan C – okay troops, we've had the affair.

Now all we have to do is tell the husband, and he'll jump back into line. Three blocks away I finally find a phone. The receiver is so heavy I can barely lift it. I feel nauseous, like I'm going to throw up. "Hello, God. Can I speak to God? . . . Are you there? . . . Is someone there?"

18

Alone

I KNOW MY mother would never have agreed to plan C. Rule number one in her book would have been never under any circumstances tell your husband the truth. But I didn't have a great Chinese web of secrets I was weaving in the back room. My secrets came out like badly mangled doilies. The doilies were too complicated to make and I was too lazy. Believing it was the more modern approach, I decided to blurt out the truth no matter who it hurt. So, in accordance with plan C, the first thing I did, when I arrived home, was tell Bobby I was having an affair too. His reaction was more dramatic than I expected.

"Jack fucked you? I'll kill him. I'll fucking kill him."

I backed up against the wall as Bobby's hands searched for something to murder. He pushed everything off the table in one sweep. Plastic dishes bounced and rolled on the floor. He grabbed the phone and threw it against the wall. Then he threw his body against the wall. Then he put his fist through the wall. I watched, detached to the point of noticing how cheaply our California home was made.

"Bobby, stop it. I wanted him to go to bed with me."

"You wanted him? Why? What was wrong with the way we made love?"

"Nothing."

"Nothing? Then I don't understand."

"Look, you cheat on me all the time, and I don't punch out the walls."

"Jesus, Molly, is that why you did this? Shit . . . SHIT." Bobby put his other hand through the wall. This place wouldn't last five minutes in a Niagara winter.

"You don't have to get so mad. I didn't have a very good time."

"What do you mean? What did he do to you? I'll kill him."

"Bobby, stop it. We're going to have to pay for that wall."

"Okay, I'm calm. Tell me what he did."

"Nothing. I just don't think I'm a very good lover, that's all."

"What are you talking about? You're great."

"But with Jack it was impossible."

"What was?"

"Well, I couldn't think of coming. I was too busy protecting myself."

"Oh God, I can't hear this. Molly, only men are good or bad lovers. The girl is only as good as the guy she's with and Jack's a fucking scumbag, he's – . Molly, you can't do this. It's just different for guys."

"Right. You mean you fuck your ass off and I should just stay home and wait for you? Bullshit, Bobby, that's bullshit."

"I'm not in love with them like I am with you."

"So, you admit it. You've been cheating on me like crazy. And those purple underpants were Jack's wife's."

While we talked on into the night, I made coffee. In the next yard over, the white trash neighbors partied to the tune of "Fear" and "White Zombie". Every once in a while a bottle would smash or someone would yell. I was beginning to like Bobby again. He was so earnest, not like the slippery eel I had for a brain. In our truth-telling session, of course, I decided against telling him anything about Kenny. It would have just confused things. It certainly confused me. The meeting in the bar with Kenny still lay like sour milk along the bottom of my stomach. I didn't know how to clean it up so I just left it there. But these things don't vanish when left alone, they get more and more rancid, and my puddle of spilt milk was increasing in size.

Bobby, on the other hand, confessed everything. He dumped each sordid tale on me like a brick. I felt so heavy I couldn't move my arms or legs. I couldn't get up from my chair. His voice dragged on brick after brick.

"I can't explain it. You're going to have to trust me on this, but it's different. I can't even remember the sex. It's just about scoring. It's like gambling. I'm telling you, when it's over, I have nothing to say to them. I come back here."

"Yeah, you come back here to change your shirt to go to the office. You probably don't even go to the office anymore."

Bobby hung his head. Then like the smooth stones from the river he used to bring me, he offered me another gift. "I got that promotion, but even better than that. Uncle Morry is retiring and I am going to run the dealership. We're going to be rich. How does that sound?"

"Great."

"You don't sound very impressed."

"I don't see how money is going to change anything."

"But I'm going to change. I'm sick of running around and I don't want to lose you. Do you think I want to end up like Jack?"

"It's not even the other girls. I just don't want to be lied to anymore. It makes me feel stupid."

"Molly, I'm through lying to you."

"Then tell the truth about something, anything. Tell me when you first cheated on me."

"Okay, but you're not going to like it."

"That's how I'll know you're telling the truth." With all this talk about fucking, Bobby had started looking sexy to me.

"Well, I never cheated on you all through high school, except the last year. I made love to an Indian girl. You don't know her." Suddenly it started snowing and I saw the Indian girl in her truck waiting for him. She was still hopelessly in love with him.

"It was a mistake, a big mistake. She got pregnant. I found out her old man owned the casino up river and he was mad, mad enough to shoot me. Your mom saved my ass. She said if you and I got married he wouldn't dare fuck with me. And then, when you came to my door wanting me to take you to LA, I figured marriage was a good idea. I promise you, I never saw the Indian girl again."

"My mother asked you to marry me?"

"I'm not saying it right. I know you hate her, but she

really was just trying to make sure you were going to be okay."

"And that's why you married me?"

"Give me a break, I've loved you since first grade. What does it matter why I married you?"

"Get out. You have to go. I'm serious. Get your things and get out."

Bobby left. There was silence . . . then a noise like a china plate falling and breaking. My mask fell off, cracking on the floor. At first I tried to glue it back with more make-up. Then, fuck it, I stopped shaving the hair on my body. By the time Christmas rolled around I was good and drunk.

Beverly Hills the week before Christmas, and all through my head, a herd of buffalo is stampeding. It's ninety-two degrees and I'm staring at mannequins dressed in fur standing in fake snow in the Swan's department store window. I'm standing here wishing it were the other way around. I wish I were standing in snow and the mannequins were sweating to death. God, I miss snow. This whole damn holiday is unnatural; Easter egg hunting, terrific. Witch-burning, where do I sign up? But Christmas? It's a cold climate holiday, and it just looks stupid in Los Angeles. You can't concentrate on sleigh bells when the Santa Ana winds are pounding down on you like a waffle iron.

Angels sway from palm trees like dressed-up rats with wings. The thought of Christmas decorations on a palm tree makes me itch. Break out in a fucking rash is more like it, and even more humiliating, it makes me line up and shop. Ugh. Shopping is like sex; it's easier to do it than explain why you don't want to. It's expected of you, it's expected of everyone. If you don't shop you could be taken away and put in the place where useless people are kept.

And so on to the true meaning of Christmas – shopping; first the sacred ritual of line-forming, look at the butt in front of you, that great display of money and power. Then ponder what is behind you, your own insignificant asshole. Fool, now, do the butt fuck, shop, fuck fuck, shop, shop.

Okay, we get the message. Outside the street is covered with snow. No, it's just glass from a ten-car collision, but I like it. At least it reminds me of snow. Down in the great cathedral mall I mumble my prayer and look for a line to get into –

The lord is my dog, I shall not want
He maketh me line up and bark
So what if my credit card runneth over
shop shop shoppp

Okay, here we are in the great God store, performing gift buying, namely buying gifts for the help and secretaries, but first let's discuss the true meaning of an expensive gift, ENVY: to remind the poorer receiver that your husband drove up in a Porsche, that he is wearing Polo, and that you, his wife, another possession, are wearing Prada (only because he would look stupid wearing it himself), and on your next face-lift he is going to cut your vocal cords if you don't shut up.

In the store, looking around, I realize I actually wish I were dead. Anything would be better than this. I am standing next to someone who looks dead, been here a week, probably is dead, but I don't give a shit because I've got to shop, got to shop, goooot to shooop. Oh, shut up. Jesus, it is crowded in here. I mean I am not alone. A herd of mindless mooing shoppers stampedes past to some batshit bargain. Maybe Swan's is finally stocking dead rats, you know, gifts for people you hate. Most of Bobby's friends are on this list, most of my friends too, for that matter. What friends? Rich people don't have friends, or maybe they do, and I'm not one of them. I hate this store. There're no clocks and nowhere to sit except in the shoe department.

Excuse me, do you stock bowling balls that latch onto and finally amputate the fingers of the bowler? I would like to order several dozen of them. Gifts of hate and rage. Tired of the ho hum thank you every Christmas? Then buy the little secretary something she really hates, something in the wrong color from Zody's or Pic 'n' Save, some piece of plastic junk that breaks in a week, something in Orlon, please, something so cheap and evil that it glows in the dark so she can't sleep . . . something that will make her face gag as she opens her box in front of him. I knew Bobby was fucking his secretary, but you know what? I didn't give a damn.

Fingering yet another jade necklace for Mom and then another even more expensive one of precious pearls and carved chunks of dark mysterious jade, I think, how many necklaces am I going to buy her to make-up for all the bad Christmases? Moms have it the worst, "Here's a vacuum cleaner, honey, or look, we bought you a dishwasher." But I don't want to start feeling sentimental remembering the proverbial ashtray I pounded out for Ma in the Alcatraz of third grade. It was probably still on the shelf in Florida along with Dad's balls and a few other scalps. There was something endearing about those homemade gifts – of course when little Kenny drew a bear ripping a child apart she didn't put that on the shelf, did she?

"Excuse me, do you have earrings to go with this necklace?"

"Madam, that's an extremely expensive necklace – "

"I don't really care about the price, do you understand. The more expensive the better. Now, show me some earrings in the same jade, and I want everything insured. It has to go to Florida." Thanks to Bobby, I'm rich, but it's too late for my monetary-minded mother to be impressed. All I can do is buy her gifts, gifts that will end up folded neatly in a sardine can forgotten on a shelf somewhere or even worse, around Kenny's neck.

By the time I get home I'm not drunk anymore. I'm getting my hangover, which I call a migraine. I take aspirin, a lot of aspirin. I worry about being alone. People will forget I'm here and I will end up dry, dry like a beetle crawling slowly over its buried possessions. If you puncture my shell a bug-like serum will ooze out instead of blood, and if someone accidentally flips me on my back I will be helpless, my legs doomed to crawl across the endless sky.

Already, I miss Bobby. I can tell because there are half eaten peanut butter sandwiches all over the place. Without him I have lost the urge to clean. Bobby left a lot of his old stuff here and I've grown to like it. I move it around in different arrangements and I talk to it too. The only problem is I can't take it to bed and don't think I haven't tried. You'll try anything when you're lonely.

I hole up for days in my messy nest. The problem with my nest, however, is that it is so messy I can't do anything in it. I can't find anything. I can't even walk across the rug anymore. All I ever do is go straight to bed, and because I go straight to bed all the time I'm never sleepy, so the only thing to do is jerk off but that's become hopeless too. There is nothing in my brain pattern that makes me feel sexy anymore and I'm afraid I've overworked that reflex so much I broke it.

So, instead I have conversations with Kenny over and over. He sits on my bed where I tell him everything I couldn't tell him in the bar.

"Crawl back in your barrel and stay there, you hear? And don't come out again unless I tell you," I scream.

"You don't know the first thing about love."

"You don't know anything about love or you couldn't have left me. You're a monster."

"Oh, that's a great excuse. And now, you come back and tell me you're gay. How long did it take you to think that one up?"

"Bullshit. I hate you. No one will ever hate you as much as I do. Do you hear me? I'll always be here hating you forever and you won't be able to forget, never, never, never. Like a rip in your flesh I will always be bleeding. You will never heal" – it ruptures in my head. The need to see blood, anyone's blood, but I am alone. I put my fingers between my teeth and bite, but it hurts too much. There are other ways – a razor, that wouldn't hurt at all. There is no one in the bathroom. I go into the white-tiled room with its watchful mirror on the wall and immediately I am aware of the need for secrecy. I must not be seen doing this. I shut the door. Self-mutilation, the words form in my brain. I am not this kind of person. Maybe I'm drinking myself to death but I'll be damned if I'm going to cut myself up too.

What the fuck am I doing in the bathroom anyway? And who shut the door? This is really scary.

I call Bobby. I tell him I just talked to Kenny. I don't tell him anything else.

"Molly, Kenny's dead. They don't have phones where he is. Maybe you're talking to him but it's not on the phone."

"Who said anything about a phone?"

"I'm trying to keep you out of a lunatic asylum."

"No, you're trying to put me there."

"Jesus, I know you're fucked up but this is ridiculous."

In the end Bobby says he will keep my credit card open as long as I go to a shrink or AA. I agreed to the terms of surrender. What does it matter? Living under the white flag, nothing matters. Fuck him. Fuck Kenny . . . fuck, fuck, fuck.

Inside my apartment the only place to go to is the bed. I curl up and immediately pass out. The bed separates me from reality, and I am surrounded by miles of dark water. There is unspeakable evil in the water. I put my hand in. It is cold but once my hand is wet, the urge to lower my whole body in is overpowering. Once I am in the water I am free. My tough gray skin and white belly feel nothing but the excitement of the water. As I swim I open my mouth and my rows of teeth ache for something to attack so that blood explodes around me like the bloom of a red rose. I am a part of this black water and I am fearless. My only problem is that when I wake up they will rip the dorsal fin off my back, seal up the gills in my throat, and ask that I return the extra sets of teeth. And I will have to walk instead of swim, but I have no legs.

Waking up in a panic, I remember, it's okay, I have legs. I can feel them. They're sticky and the sheets are spotted with blood. The razor that has always been in the bathroom is now sitting on the night table next to the clock. Jumping out of bed I examine my body everywhere. There are several small cuts on my legs. I examine my body again – nothing else. My shark has turned against me, and I didn't even see the attack.

The next morning is overcast and cold. I huddle on my bed as if I was on a raft. I know I'm drifting. I should grab hold of something but there is nothing to hang on to.

I'm so lonely, I break down and call Ma. Kenny answers, "Hello?"

"Hello . . ."

"Mei Li?"

"Bobby thinks you're a hallucination because I drink too much. There really is a fifty-fifty chance that I might be going bonkers and that you're not real." There is no answer on the other end. "So I thought I'd call up and find out . . . if you're real." I don't know what I expected. I thought he might laugh. I know I was close to crying. But neither of those things happened. Kenny's voice was dead serious and it sobered me so much I answered him as if we were brother and sister again and none of this had happened.

"You got to come down here. I can't do this by myself."

"Kenny, what's wrong?"

"She's in the hospital again. She's got to go into a home."

"I'll be there tomorrow. As soon as I can get a reservation."

"Okay. Hurry."

19

Chinese lunch

GETTING A PLANE to Florida was not as easy as I thought it would be. My credit card came back carefully snipped in half. I was overdrawn and had no cash, which meant I had to ask Bobby for money. This morning I don't drink. I carefully apply make-up to the girl in the mirror. I examine her teeth to make sure they are still human. I wash them several times and after each time I redo my lipstick. Every Wednesday I have to meet Bobby for lunch. Needless to say, lunch is very important since it is the only thing we share that goes in and out of our bodies now that we don't have sex. He says it's to catch up. I know it's to check up on me and decide whether or not to cancel my credit card.

Bobby looks good, although he seems to have gained a bit of weight around his waist, but the cut of the suit covers it nicely. As the owner of the dealership, Bobby has blossomed from dark obsessive pack rat into a bright happy consumer. Now he buys Japanese suits, antiques, art. I don't know where he gets the good taste from, but

I guess it's from whomever he's balling at the time of purchase. I'm sure she's very rich and chic, and impressed that he drives around in a red corvette wearing designer shades. Meanwhile, I suffer from lack of appetite or as my shrink would have put it, lack of sex.

My shrink was very into sex. Men don't like it when they see a girl not being fucked by someone, anyone. That's why "virgin" is such a dirty word in this culture. After Jack I became gun-shy, it was ridiculous. I had gone from sexually precocious teen to stumbling shy spinster in just one affair, and I had the uncomfortable feeling that my shrink was bored because I didn't have any sexual problems to tell him. I couldn't believe I was worried about entertaining him. It was humiliating, so I fired him.

Bobby, of course, never went to the shrink with me because he's a perfectly well-balanced human being. In other words he's sane and I'm not. In retaliation I have never told him about seeing Kenny because it makes me feel like the sane one to have this bit of information on him. The real reason he can't see a shrink is he doesn't have time. He's too busy "working," which is code for cheating on his newest girlfriend. No one ever knows where he is because he's surrounded by a gaggle of secretaries who constantly lie about his whereabouts. At the moment he looks pissed off and I assume the worst, that he's found out I dumped the shrink.

"Your credit card has a debit of several grand."

"I bought a Christmas gift for Ma." I wait for the lecture on spending too much money.

Bobby stares back at me. "That's really nice of you," he says. He means it.

The air conditioning of the little Chinese restaurant, if they ever had it, is broken and I feel sticky. Bobby sits in front of me eating happily while I try to look nonchalant, something completely foreign to my Asian nature. Instead of looking at the menu I watch the trapped fish bumping their heads against the plastic sides of the cheap aquarium. Every Wednesday it's the Bob thing, the Bob restaurant, the Bob menu. Pick out your fish and we cook it – only the Chinese could think of such a barbaric custom. I twist the wedding ring on my finger and look up at Bobby.

"I have to go see Ma, and I need money for the ticket."

"What's wrong with her?"

"She's crazy, that's all."

"Nothing hereditary, I hope."

"I see, I'm your crazy Chinese wife now. Something you have to put away out of sight."

"It was just a joke."

"My sense of humor, small as it is, has gotten even smaller. She's in the hospital."

"I'm sorry. Go to Florida. I'll take care of the ticket."

"Thank you." When Bobby is supportive like this, it confuses me.

"By the way, how is your psychiatrist?"

"I don't see Mr Shrink anymore."

"I thought we had a deal. You see the shrink, I pay the bills."

"Look, the shrink was a fucking moron. All he wanted to talk about was my mother. I don't hate my mother. I wish I did, it would be easier. I love her. Like some featherless duck, I imprinted on the first thing I saw which unavoidably was Ma. Perhaps there is some emotional toggle switch on an unreachable place along my backbone that makes me love her no matter how much documentation I pile up on the injustices she is responsible for. I mean where is that toggle switch – just let me get my hands on it and I can start living a normal life. You know what he said? He said everyone hates their mother – that's why men hate women, but because women are female they have to hate themselves."

"What do you want for dessert?" Bobby hates to talk about shrink stuff. He just wants to know I'm going, I'm being fixed, I'll be ready soon.

"And I don't hate myself. I mean, okay. I drink, but I drink to feel good not because I hate myself."

"You said you wanted to go to lunch, and when we get here, you don't eat. Are you going to eat that?"

Pushing what I am sure is a genetically engineered shrimp around the plate in small circles I don't answer him. I'm thinking of having eye surgery just to annoy him. The only reason he comes to this crappy Chinese restaurant is because I'm Asian. He thinks it will impress them that he has a Chinese wife. They know I'm only half-Chinese and I hate their food. The restaurant is in a poor area, and we stick out like a sore thumb, but for some reason being the only round eyes in an Asian restaurant confirms the authenticity of the food for Bobby. I feel like a fake. Maybe if I had my tongue pierced, that would wake Bobby up. I feel like I'm on display along with the flat pink fish sadly floating out their last hours in plastic tanks next to the lobsters who wait on top of each other for their boiling death, their claws clamped shut by rubber bands.

Proud of the freshness of their fish, the waiter lifts

another helpless meal out of its tank and carries it off into the kitchen where its head will be lopped off by a crazed chef. I always expect someone to rise from his table and point an accusing finger at me while saying something I can't understand. Then the waiter will carry me to the kitchen, and lay me on the metal table, where our sadistic chef will slit my throat and hang me upside down to slowly bleed to death. Bobby will mutter, "Well done." No, no, he means he wants her well done, and that will be the end of it. The papers will carry a small blurb, "Man eats his wife," and some people will snicker at the sexual innuendo saying, "What a woman has to go through to get off these days."

The waiter takes my food away with a concerned look on his face. This is the part of the meal I dread the most, where Bobby insists on having an after-dinner conversation with our waiter, not a simple hello, how are you, that would be fine, but an in-depth conversation. The concern Bobby has wasted on this stupid little man who doesn't understand much more than spoon and napkin infuriates me.

Unable to cover my boredom I long to slip under the table and join the lobsters who managed to escape. Surely not all were going to die. Some knew a secret way out, and I would follow them in their slow ancient march along the carpeted floor out into the grassy sunlight. The idea of black lobsters dancing on the grass in their cryptic pointy fashion is the only thing that gets me through these paralytic conversations.

It's more than ridiculous. It's unnatural. Bobby is the head of a very large car dealership. The idea of the boss, as the waiter calls him, trying to make friends with a harried little waiter doesn't just embarrass me, it clearly embarrasses the confused waiter. Bobby also tips him exorbitantly, certainly too much for someone just off the boat. With comical confusion the little waiter tries to refuse the money, but Bobby won't hear of it, patiently explaining that it's the company's money. Everyone is bought in LA — that is the way. Still, this yellow man insists on trying to balance the scales with gifts of his own. To my disgust Bobby takes each one as a precious sign of some male bonding that he's afraid to look for in normal relationships. Bobby accepts the cheap red plastic good luck symbol, hanging it from the car mirror like some red wound that I half expect to start leaking blood. It is the same color as Ma's red fingernails flashing in the lights.

Instead of saying anything, I join the lobsters, my hands clamped shut on the linen tablecloth as if bound by heavy rubber bands, seaweed tangled around my ankles, holding me to the floor, while the waiter bobs up and down like a cork. Bobby shifts in his chair. He's uneasy when things do not go as he thinks they should. The boss insists the waiter pull up a chair, and I watch them fumble on the language barrier. The earrings on my ear itch, even the dress on my back threatens to shed like the skin of a reptile. They're all things Bobby has bought me, and they all remind me of purple underpants. Why couldn't this waiter shut up and take his money like I did? Then Bobby could feel at ease, in control, worthy. I'm going to be sick.

In spite of the sweet sesame cakes that we always end our meal with, gall rises in my throat like green liver blossoming in the lobster's white meat. Suddenly my voice ricochets across the dining room, "What do you want from him? He's just a waiter." My laughter shatters the air like shrapnel hitting the china, and Bobby involuntarily raises his hand against it.

In a small boy's voice, he answers, "I want to learn."

"What?" I shriek, irritation erupting along the canals of my brain like a mini lava flow.

"I thought you liked it here . . ." continued Bobby.

"Why? Because I'm Asian? He's a waiter, a fucking waiter, not the reincarnation of the Buddha."

His hand closes over my knee to silence me and I push it away. The waiter quietly runs for the cover of the kitchen but I still cannot hold my tongue, "That waiter doesn't understand you. He's not ever going to be your friend no matter how much you tip him. You're wearing a two-thousand-dollar suit and you're talking to waiters. Wake up."

"Molly, what are you saying?"

"What am I saying? What are we doing? I want a divorce."

"What? I thought we made a commitment, for better or worse."

"We have insurmountable problems."

"We're working on them."

"Why bother? We don't even live together."

"Because I love you."

"Well, it's not enough. If you loved me you would be fucking me."

"Lower your voice. Nothing is enough for you."

This stops me for a second as Bobby continues in a tense voice. "Did it ever cross your mind that love is a decision you make and stick to?"

"Is that the deal you made with my mother?"

"No. Molly, it means I'm not giving you up."

"What makes you think it's your decision?"

Bobby's eyes almost cross in confusion. He's trying to be the romantic lead but the idea of losing me for good is frustrating him. His voice sputters like the fuse on a stick of dynamite. "I'm not going to abandon you, not when you need help."

"Oh right, I'm the sick one. You haven't the faintest idea what love is. It's not decision-making and it's not a fucking score card, it's passion."

The dynamite blows. "Like the passion you and Kenny had?"

"What is that supposed to mean? What's my brother have to do with this?" I look for shelter from what is coming next, but there is none.

"He told me he fucked you. Like a dog, that's how he said it. Like a dog, he fucked you in your old tree house."

"You mean all this time you knew?"

"He told me everything, how you said you would always love him, how you looked, and how you felt, what he did to you. He said it all with a smirk, until I couldn't stand it anymore, and I hit him." Bobby's voice was toneless as if he was reciting something he had been forced to memorize. "I hit him. It was like hitting a vacuum. He wouldn't fight back. He tried to kiss my hands. It made me so angry I hit him again. He wanted me to hit him. He kept on saying it over and over and I hit him over and over, but he wouldn't stop saying it."

Kenny's bleeding face floated in front of me as Ma's red nails held it up to the lamp light. I remembered crying, but Kenny wasn't crying. He was smiling. Smiling like when we played under the tree and he was the knight dying on the battlefield. I had to spend hours dressing his make-believe wounds, after which he would die anyway.

"Saying what?" Saying, I love you as Bobby smashed his face in again and again, and I can't help him because it has already happened.

Bobby's eyes looked at me like a cornered dog and then the snarl came, "So you see, Molly, you were the first to cheat. You can't blame me for being angry. For wanting to hurt you back, so I cheated on you with the Indian girl – and I'm still cheating on you, trying to punish you."

"You lying sack of shit. You're blaming all this on me. You fuck everyone in the world and it's my fault? You bastard . . . you fucking bastard. You were sucking my brother's dick the whole time."

He put his hand out to stop the words from coming out of my mouth, as if words were something he could catch and push back down my throat when I bit him. If I had thought about it I could never have done it, but I bit him right down to the bone. I tasted his blood and felt my teeth sink through his flesh, and I didn't close my eyes either. Instead I shook my head like a cat does when it bites into something. I turn and make another pass at him. This time his leg comes off in my mouth. His blood blossoms into the water like a gigantic black rose intoxicating me with the sheer pleasure. It has nothing to do with eating anymore. I don't even care if anything is in my mouth. I just want to smell the blood and gnash my teeth in ecstasy.

We spend the next five hours in a hospital. On the way home I watch the lights go by in the semi-blackness that passes for LA nights, like neon phosphorescent fish –

ghostly white ones, quick green ones, and schools of tiny red ones up ahead. "I'm lost in a school of mindless fish being pulled by an unknown current."

"That's very poetic but what you really are is drunk."

"I'm not drunk enough. I drink to get numb and stop this from happening."

Bobby has to let me drive. While he sits cradling his bandaged hand, he talks quietly. He says he'll give me a divorce even though he didn't want one. He says it like I've won, but Niagara is not pounding in my ears. Instead there is only silence. I'm not sure if I wanted this victory.

"So, Kenny is alive."

"Yeah, I'm sorry to disappoint you but my brother is alive and well, and you're the one who is in a slight bit of denial here."

"You are so angry and I've never known why."

"You mean people have to have reasons to get angry?"

"Most people do." He smiles sadly and we drive in silence, Bobby and his pet shark. I can just see us if we stay together: Bobby will be missing several fingers and maybe a foot or two.

"You know, I used to hope his death was a joke. That he would call me up and we would laugh about it. But I never got that call."

"Don't feel bad. No one got that call."

"Have you been seeing him?"

"No, he lives in Florida. He's gay."

"No shit." Bobby chuckled to himself.

"What?"

"You wasted your whole life being in love with him."

"I didn't waste it. I enjoyed it. So it's not a waste."

"Okay, you wasted my life. Because you love him, not me. There, I said it. Can you tell me I'm wrong? Can you say you love me?"

The neon fish are sliding by faster and faster, but now they are familiar. I have driven to my house and now I want Bobby to come inside with me. "Sure, I love you. You want me to say it again?"

"You love me . . . not him?"

"Look, you can't drive home. Come inside."

"I can drive if I have to. I'll have my secretary arrange your ticket tomorrow."

"Thanks."

Bobby looks lost, like the kid I used to know. "You ever hear Niagara, or think you hear it — far away? I do. I can hear it now."

"Bobby, please stay with me tonight."

That night we slept together, but I didn't make love with the sexy blond kid from Niagara. That kid had slipped through my fingers and I was making love to someone else. The motions were the same but they were ever so slightly premeditated, as if Bobby were searching for that kid too. It was too crowded to find anyone. Although I lay in Bobby's arms, we were not alone. There were other shadowy people in his head, women, wanting to stake a claim, to have a piece of whatever was left of the beautiful football hero. He was being eaten alive. So, I held his head and told him it was great, a reassurance he never needed before. I didn't lash out in my normal smart-ass style and say, you've fucked around so much the act is no longer attached to the emotion and your dick is totally confused. For once I just lay beside him quietly.

I had been so busy rejecting Bobby, I never paid

attention to how handsome he had grown up to be. But gods come to earth for only a short glimpse of time, and Bobby's good looks must have hung over his head like the sword of Damocles. He must have known it was temporary and people wanted him for what he represented to them not for who he was. I think he was happy to climb back into his fat Bobby shell where it was safe. Then it hit me . . . I understood why Bobby was in love with me and would be for the rest of his life. I was the only one he trusted. I was the girl that was different from all the others. I liked him when he was fat and he assumed I would love him now that he was a car dealer with a gut that was threatening to get wider.

As a matter of fact the other Bobby scared me as much as it did him. The other Bobby, that incredible body bleeding black blood in the blue moonlight as he stepped casually over his fallen victim, that was something that could only be worshiped, not loved. So I did believe Bobby when he said he only wanted me. He needed me, that I understood. I could do that job. He was right to trust me. I pressed against his belly and kissed his chest the way Kenny and I kissed our swords in the chapel of trees, "To the death, to the death," is what we would whisper over the roar of the Falls.

"Bobby, I don't want a divorce. I want a honeymoon."

For one breathtaking minute I thought he was going to tell me to get lost. Then the old sheepish hopefulness returned to his eyes, "You do?"

"Yeah, why not? We never had one. So, let's go when I get back." Snuggling closer to him, I can feel a happy warmth radiating from his body. This is what I need. I'm so tired of being cold. Back and forth, back and forth swims my shark. Perhaps I can shut it up in an aquarium of sorts, behind some thick safety glass like you see in the zoo.

20

My brother

KENNY MET ME at the airport. This time he wore a boy's get-up, a heavy metal tee-shirt, tight black pants with a lot of zippers, and large Frankenstein boots. His hair was flame red and spiked. It's amazing how quickly the bizarre becomes familiar: because after about ten minutes I had trouble imagining him looking any different. He drove us directly to the hospital, talking all the way. This Kenny was different than the moody one I grew up with and different than the hissing cobra I met in the bar. He couldn't shut up.

"Ma can't take care of herself. She's got walking pneumonia. I don't know how she got it. I take care of her the best I can, but it's not good enough. She has to go into an assisted living facility, but she won't go. She's afraid to leave her house. You have to declare her insane and have her put in a home."

"I can't do that."

"You have to. It's just a formality. You're the only one who can. You're her daughter. You also have to get power of attorney and prevent all that money from going to a lot of fat greedy Buddhist monks."

"You really have been thinking about this."

"They're on her like flies and they steal stuff. I caught one walking out with a lampshade.

"That can't be right. Monks give up all material possessions."

"Yeah well, I'm telling you, these monks are different. They eat the food I buy her. They go in the refrigerator when I'm not looking."

"You've seen them do this?"

"No, I just told you. They do it when I'm not looking."

Kenny was sounding like the one I should declare insane. "What are you worried about, Ma or her money?"

"Unfair. I'm the one who has been stuck down here taking care of her. I don't want to complain, but everyone in this town is over ninety. Even the police are old farts. No one drives over thirty miles an hour."

"I'm sorry. That was the wrong thing to say. I want to help."

"Wow, you're being awfully adult for a princess."

"I don't want to fight."

"Okay. Let's just talk about Ma. You're the strong one here. You've got to put her in a home."

"Strong? Me? Look at my life."

"Okay, you're angry. It's the same thing."

"Why can't she stay where she is?"

"Do you know why she left Niagara?"

"The weather."

"No, the embarrassment. She left because she couldn't remember the cards anymore. She didn't want anyone to know her mind was going. She came out here to die so she wouldn't be a problem for anyone, except dying is a long slow process. In her case it's going to take years."

The back of my throat tightened to think of Ma, alone, covering the encroaching decay with bits of newspaper, knowing her mind was going, her fierce pride hanging in the closet with her old mink eaten away by moths. Writing notes to herself to remember where the telephone was and how to use it, what the microwave was for and how to use it. What Tuesday was for and how to use it.

At the hospital the nurses and staff greeted Kenny as if everyone in Florida dressed that way. He was obviously a favorite around here. Opening the door to Ma's room he lowered his voice, "Molly, don't be freaked out if she doesn't know who you are."

Inside, Ma was doing something I had never seen her do, watching TV. She looked over at me and smiled to the nurse, "Connie Chung, come in. The news is just beginning."

As my tears start, Kenny pulls me into the waiting room because Connie Chung isn't supposed to just stand there and cry.

"She doesn't remember me. I'm too late. Why didn't you tell me?"

"What did you think was going on down here?"

"I don't know. I thought – you said you'd take care of – I wasn't thinking." I started crying for real. Not for Ma, I'm sorry to say, but for me, because I lost something important and it was my own fault. I left her here. I didn't take care of her. I made sure Kenny was stuck with the job. I was the bad person. I didn't deserve a mother. Something was lost and I couldn't find her. I remembered my father, obsessed with searching the river for objects the Falls had stolen. Did he think he could find what he was looking for, or was going through the motion just as important? Or is it all just so fucking sad, you don't give up looking because that's the only relief?

"Don't cry, little sister. Mornings are much better for her. She'll know who you are. It's in the evening that the people in the TV come and visit her."

"Is it going to get worse?"

"Of course it's going to get worse, it's progressive. This fucking doctor says the last stages are barking and biting. But don't worry. You don't have to buy a leash and collar yet."

"Kenny, that's not funny."

"Oh yes, it is. If you don't keep a sense of humor going this could all be real depressing."

"She's so little, like a puppet. Why did we think she was a dragon?"

"It's okay, Molly. All we have to do is find her a nice cave to live in."

The afternoon sun spills happily into the waiting room, completely unaware that the people here are suffering. I think Kenny is on drugs. He talks all the time, but I like it. As he talks, his words begin to build a safety net so I don't go drifting off on the little eddies and currents of pain that swirl out of each room and rush down the hallways.

"I never thought Ma was a dragon." His voice drowns out the whispers leaking from the other rooms. "She saved my life because I came that close to taking it. Growing up in Niagara, I thought I was going crazy at one point, in a backwoods school that hates Jews, niggers, and fags, and I'm leading this double life, doing my classmates at night, but in the day they don't mention it, like it never happened. She's the only one who figured it out."

"How did she know when I didn't?"

"Ma had a whole other life before she came here and, from what I can gather, it was pretty decadent. Anyway, homosexuality wasn't anything new to her. She talked to me about it, so I didn't think I was the only person in the world who felt the way I did. That kept me sane. You kept me sane too, but in a different way. You were the only other person who really did love me back then." This was the old Kenny. This was how his voice sounded, when Niagara purred underneath it. The silky laughing voice that could talk me into anything.

"Love you? I didn't know who you were," I whisper back.

"Yes, you did. You didn't know everything, but so what? Don't you remember the tree house and the sound of Niagara in the background? You used to love that sound. You said it talked to you."

"Come on, Kenny, you were just using me to keep Bobby around," I answer halfheartedly.

"Yeah, I used you. That doesn't mean I didn't love you. You see, there was no place for me, so I had to make one. I never meant to hurt you. I was always very careful with you."

"It was the best time of my life, Kenny. Isn't that pathetic?"

"It was the worst time for me. I need a martini."

"What happened to AA?"

Kenny shrugs his shoulders and grins. "I usually smuggle a bottle in. They haven't caught me yet." Kenny pulls out a half full bottle of vodka. I am happy to know I won't be drinking alone. "Here's to life in San Diego."

"San Bernardino."

"You don't sound very happy about it."

"I don't think I'm capable of being happy. Other people are happy, but I haven't quite got the hang of it." Kenny grins. He is the only person I could ever say this to who would know what I was talking about. It makes me feel good to know that my past is locked safely in this boy's head, so as long as he is around I won't misplace it. I won't lose it like I lose my mother sometimes to the airwaves of the television.

By the way, how is Bobby?"

"He says he's not going to cheat on me."

"That'll be the day." Kenny laughs.

"I don't care."

"Now, don't lie to elder brother. You love Bobby."

Kenny is right, Ma is better in the mornings. But she is only half there. In a way she is the child now and I am the mother. Only this mother is going to put her baby in an institution. The next day the same sun continues to pour into the waiting room and we are feeling quite toasty, yes indeedy. As a matter of fact, we are very close to being drunk. A nurse comes in and I figure we're going to get busted for cocktails, but she just smiles and pats Kenny on the shoulder like he was her pet hamster. As soon as she leaves, Kenny continues to fill in the rest of our past, the shadow part that followed me around, the part I never knew about.

"In the school shower after football practice it was forbidden to get a hard-on. I never got one, but poor fucking Paul Jones did and from then on he was ostracized as Boner Jones."

"I remember Boner. He was sad. We all hated him but I never knew that was the reason."

"He became the school whipping boy for everything queer. It was really unfair. While I gave boys the eye and did them in the back of the gym, Boner caught everyone's shit for the rest of his school career."

"When did you start . . . doing boys?"

Kenny rolls his eyes. "What do you think the club house was for? I supplied the cigarettes, beer and the dirty magazines. We'd talk about looking for trouble, talk about sex. Sometimes they wouldn't want it. I'd put my hand on their leg. I could tell."

I tried to imagine Kenny going into the drug store, where he was known, to buy copies of *Penthouse*. He must have stolen the booze from Dad, stocking his little trap in order to catch some moments of that forbidden excitement that made him so different from everyone else. The loneliness of what Kenny was telling me was like a lead ceiling crushing my skull. It wasn't so much what he did, as the fact that he had to face it all alone. "You were so young to be doing that."

"From what I remember, Princess, you were pretty sexually active at a young age too."

The idea that I didn't know any of this was going on made me feel like shit. It made me think Kenny was right; I was some kind of princess with my head up my ass. I waited for the shark to slice through the confusing alcoholic fog that was bringing my brain to a standstill, but it didn't happen. I didn't get angry. The more out of it I was, the more I wanted to hear. "So, the fake death was just to get back at Dad?"

"My death? No, I put the barrel in the river as a joke, princess, that's all. I thought you'd get it." Kenny smiled slyly. "But when everyone believed I was in the bloody thing, it became my ticket out."

"But you planned it, all those months of barrel building."

"I didn't plan to kill myself, just shock everyone. Every day I was going to go back and say, here I am, it was just a joke, but I didn't. And each day that I didn't go back, it got harder and harder. Then, it just got too hard. I was going to write a letter, but even that was too hard."

"I thought you were having a good laugh about everyone crying around your grave."

"No, it made me feel ashamed. Too ashamed to call any of you. So then I couldn't go home, but I guess that's what I wanted. I had to get out of there. I was turning into a chicken hawk."

"A chicken hawk? What's that?"

"An old guy who goes after young boys."

"You were only nineteen. That's not old."

"Eric Shleszer's brother was four years younger than me. He was fifteen."

"Did you?"

"No, but I thought about it. Shit, I thought for sure they were going to chase me out of town like Frankenstein. I used to dream about it. And with good reason because by sixteen I had busted all the macho acts on the football team and I was going after their younger brothers."

"Why?"

"I wanted to take away their innocence, like mine was taken from me."

I didn't know what to say. The dinner trays were clattering in the background. The sun was setting behind windows that never opened. For a minute I was scared, then Kenny started talking again and I heard Niagara purring in the distance.

"You know I went back. None of those guys wanted to see me. They're all married with children now and, let's just say, I make them nervous. They can't have the little woman thinking they're queer. Of course, who knows what they do on their lunch breaks."

"What guys?"

"There were five of us when I started school. We played sex games, and I pretty much knew what to do. By the time we were in high school they were your typical jocks, but they were used to me sucking their dicks and they didn't want to give it up. So we kept it up. It was a very zip and unzip affair. Other boys used me too when their girlfriends wouldn't put out. After a night of heavy petting but no nooky they would call me around midnight and ask if I wanted to take a drive with them. Even if I was in bed asleep, I would get up and go with them. Bobby was the only one who didn't treat me like a leper, dropping me off blocks from my house, or pushing my head under the dashboard so they weren't seen with me. He was always a friend first, whether I sucked his dick or not. Am I being too graphic for you?"

"No."

"I learned that in a weird way I was very powerful, because the guys were so afraid I would tell on them. It was like blackmail. After I called one of them a cock-sucker, nobody dared fuck with me. People were afraid of me, but I wasn't afraid of them. Couple the insult of homosexuality with their biggest flaw – that they were ugly, or the son of a farmer, awkward or stupid – yell that out loud when there's a crowd around and the most macho guys shrink to nothing." Kenny was into it. I'm sure he had told the nurses his life story too. That's why they were forever being so fucking nice to him. "Even the teachers, I called out that prick of a coach, Val shoots blanks is what I'd yell at him. He was a veteran and the girls said he couldn't get his wife pregnant. That bastard sent me home for playing dirty. And I did play dirty. I had to. I'd go for the knees, step on their hands. I had to. Remember Dad insisting I play center. Shit, I was the only fag in Niagara and I didn't even weigh ninety pounds."

"You had Bobby to back you up."

"You know he beat me up?"

"I know. He told me about it."

Now, it was Kenny's turn to be surprised, "He did? What did you do, go home and blab to him?"

"I called him a cock-sucker just like you told me not to," I said with a smile.

"So, what did he say? Tell me. Tell me." Kenny's eyes were all hungry and excited at the same time. I could feel my shark watching from the other side of an aquarium glass like a cat watches a mouse.

"He just smiled and said, So Kenny's alive. Then he said he thought you would have phoned or something.

You should probably come out to LA. He would like to see you."

"I can't, I have friends here."

"So, bring your friend, just for a visit." Why was I saying this when I knew it wasn't going to happen? I knew I didn't want Kenny in LA. But I had to suggest the one thing I didn't want.

Kenny's eyes got moist and he practically purred in happiness, "Maybe just a tiny visit after we get Ma settled."

21

The home

THE PLAN WAS to take Ma straight from the hospital to
the home and tell her it was temporary. The home was
called Midway Manor. I don't know what the End of
the Line Manor looked like but Midway was too white,
too clean, and too damn utilitarian. Everything
including the flowers were brightly colored and plastic
so they could be easily washed. Everyone had their own
TV and they were encouraged to watch it. So long as
they were facing the TV they were "okay." So what
if they were drooling over their jammies? So what if
their heads were in their soup? So what if they were
discussing something with no one? Their hearts were
beating, that's all the state of Florida needed.

Kenny, Ma, and I were being driven in a golf cart to
the dining area. Ma sat like a small child between her
two insane new parents: Kenny, who had toned down
his dress to a pink shirt and neon green iridescent pants,
and me, who came prepackaged in solid black. We did
agree on one thing. We all wore giant sunglasses. We

were a family again, even if we did look like the three blind mice.

"He's drunk, Ma. He was drinking at breakfast."

"She doesn't care." Kenny grins at Ma and gives her a hug. She grins back like a twelve-year-old on her way to Disneyland.

"And you were giving me all this shit about AA when you met me in that bar."

"AA was good. I wish I was still in it." As he talks his eyes get that distant sad look. It wasn't the response I was looking for.

"Really? You liked all that apologizing?"

Kenny shrugs and doesn't answer.

"When you talked to Dad before he died, did you apologize?"

This crack gets a rise out of him. "Our great war hero, Dad the coward, the drunk, and the fool." Kenny waited a moment for the sarcasm in his voice to subside. "You know, I apologized for the one time I got thrown out of our local bar for trying to pick up my first guy in a rest room. The one time I tried a stranger and Dad happened to be in the bar. And what does our Dad do? He pretends he's too drunk to recognize me, that's what he does. He just sits there while they throw me out. Yeah, I apologized for that and you know what he said. He said he beat the guy up. Not the guys who threw me out – the poor transient I tried to pick up. He followed that poor bastard out of the bar and beat him up for trying to turn his son into a homo."

This is where I knew I was my father's child because the idea of my brother kneeling before some sack of shit stranger made my blood boil and I wanted to punch him out too. I put my hands through my hair and groaned.

"It wasn't that bad, Sis," Kenny laughed. "What he really wanted to do was beat me up, but that's as far as he got."

Both Ma and I wait for this story to evaporate. Like poison gas it clings to everything. The golf cart takes a while to outrun it.

"Didn't Dad say anything else to you?"

"You mean like a father–son moment? No, he didn't say anything to me before he died. He hated me."

"No," Ma piped up, "he was afraid for you to be gay."

"I'd rather he hated me, Ma. The other is too sad."

"Yes, sad and just gets sadder. Then, breaks open like a big egg and suddenly not alone, all sadness understood connecting everybody together."

Kenny and I look at each other. Kenny shakes his head, "Now she's a philosopher?"

"Ma, not everything is a big egg," I tell her. "She used to tell me a man's ego is like a snake's egg."

"I never told you that. I like eggs. Mango makes me sad so I can't eat. But eggs, I can eat."

"If you had teeth, Ma, you could eat."

"No, I don't want teeth. I want to go home. Kenny?"

"Come on, Ma, what about the egg salad lunch we promised you?"

"Okay. But then can we go home?"

"Sure, Ma. Sure."

The dining area is a large pink room with turquoise tablecloths. In the center of each table is a bowl of orange cheese doodles. Each person has a plastic champagne glass of cherry liquid that matches the Christmas decorations that remain up throughout the year. We are told it is because the decorations are so cheerful but in reality, they are a blinking danger sign indicating that no one in this room knows what time of year it is. The inmates, whose only crime is being older than the world has use for, are having a party. I'm not sure they are aware of that either.

When Kenny and I leave, it is without Ma. We have lied to her. We didn't go to Midway Manor for a lunch of egg salad. We went to drop off our mother, like a bundle of laundry. Could you please take care of this? It's not very big so it shouldn't cost much. When we left her, there was no fight, no harsh words, no tears, just more lies about how we were coming back and maybe I would move to Florida so Ma could go back home. I tried to justify it: she left me, now years later I leave her, but that just made it seem worse. The old pain echoed through my body, nailing my stomach to my backbone.

Kenny turns out to be the sensitive one, remembering photographs, a deck of cards, selecting her clothes. While I deal with the bills, the lawyer, and the government, Kenny plays house. He treats her like a big doll and she loves it. Back and forth, back and forth my shark swims, waiting for the glass in the aquarium to crack. This time the target is Kenny instead of Ma. It's the same old pattern, I feel left out. I wait around awkwardly while he gives them instructions about her hair. He has even bought a bottle of red nail polish for her to take to the beauty parlor area. Everything here is an area, as if they were expecting a big silver plane to come and carry them away, a sweet silver chariot to finally take them home.

On the way out a nurse smiles patiently. Our problem

is not special to her. She sees it every day. "It's for her own good," she says. "After a month they love it so much they never want to leave." She's lying too. I know it. "She'll be calling bingo before you know it." The idea of Ma, Niagara's greatest gambler, calling bingo stuns me. The nurse goes on bleating like a goat, "She'll be having affairs. You'd be surprised. We have quite a few affairs going on here. There's one woman, she's so cute, she's ninety-four, and she has two boyfriends. Of course, they don't do anything. They can barely get out of their chairs, but they're in love." The nurse laughs and I want to shove all the plastic flowers down her throat. I want to cut open her pink skin so that her white uniform resembles a field of crimson roses. I think of calling Falling Water and telling him where Ma is. I know she hasn't told him. She's too proud to have him see her here. He won't be coming down and holding her hand and telling her he loves her. Someone should and I can't.

Driving back to the motel, Kenny and I try to joke around but it falls flat. I know the ocean is lying around here somewhere, waiting for my mother to forget how to swallow and finally how to breathe. I am thankful for the way the Floridians have decided to cement over most of their state in the same fashion that Ma spread newspapers around, to cover up all signs of advancing decay. Having dispatched Ma, Kenny and I are like two bookends with no books in between, useless and out of place. This has put both of us in a bad mood. Bad enough that I end up asking the one question I instinctively know I should avoid.

"Kenny?"

"What?"

"Is Bobby gay?"

"Sounds like he's too busy fucking women to find out. But that's what they're all worried about, isn't it?" A little sarcastic laugh escapes from his throat like a small snake darting out of a hole. "Isn't it?" He insists.

"What?"

"Isn't that what you're worried about? Isn't that why you flew all the way down here?"

"Fuck you." The glass shatters. For a moment nothing happens, but I know it's coming. I know the shark is loose and traveling like a locomotive towards its victim.

Kenny and I stop talking. It's as if we're the only people on the planet. Every one else drives by in their air-conditioned cars, locked in their own world, sealed off in their own heads. It's amazing that they have no idea how terrible I feel. I hate them. I hate everyone. I drop Kenny off at his motel.

"Okay, Sis. Cocktails at the Beachcomber."

"No, I have to pack. I'm leaving tonight. There's nothing left to keep me here."

Kenny's first instinct is to smile his best sarcastic smile, "And here I thought we were bonding."

"You think I've forgiven you and we're going to be one big happy family now? Well, you're wrong. I'm leaving you, just like you left me. Remember?"

"If you're doing this to get even, Molly, it's a bad idea."

As I throw the car into gear something breaks in Kenny's face. I know he is finished running. He is going to stay in Florida, but I'm not.

"You bitch, I can't believe you're doing this. Go on

then, go. Nice try, but you don't love anybody but yourself." As the car pulls away from Kenny, his whole body and face undergo a change as if his nervous system has been shuffled like a deck of cards. The last thing he says is, "Molly, I love you."

I didn't listen to the last sentence. I didn't even look at him as I drove away. It wasn't until I was halfway down the block that I thought I heard him yell, "Molly, I love you." But that might have been in my head.

The first mile or two I feel nothing. The decision to leave was pure impulse and I don't want to think about whether I was right or wrong or happy or sad. I just want to drive with the freedom of not knowing where I'm going. Driving in the humid Florida night air, it's like being underwater. The yellow from the setting sun mixes with the dark blue of oncoming night and turns the sky green. Against this neon green the palm trees stand in black silhouette. To my horror, I can feel my shark swimming next to me. I step on the gas. I will never be rid of this creature. I know it's going to follow me back to LA, looking for its next victim. Who will it be, Bobby or me? That's an evil question. So I hope it's me instead of Bobby. Is that love when you hope for something like that? I like to think so. Looking up I find that I have driven back to my motel. Inside, I make plane reservations. I pack. I repack. I drive to the airport and wait.

There is no question about it, I have made the worst mistake of my life. It's so incredibly unspeakable that I can't move. There is a bank of telephones in front of me, but I don't make the call to tell Kenny he was right, the more I found out about him the more I loved him. The idea of little Kenny setting traps in the forest of junior high for five minutes of sexual pleasure to fill his empty emotional landscape sends me into a tailspin of sympathy far more powerful than the fantasy love I was acting out in our tree house, and I can't move. I'm going to call but every minute I don't makes it harder and harder. They announce my plane. An hour has gone by and I still haven't called. I can't.

On the plane I have time to think. My departure was a clean mental break on my part, not muddied by emotion. It's a decision I made and carried out and, I tell myself, I performed it correctly. Kenny is right, I am the strong one. The operation has relieved me of all excess baggage, freeing me to begin again, to look forward to my second honeymoon. These are the excuses you make up when you have none. These are the excuses you tell yourself when you have made the wrong choice, because brothers don't grow on trees and I had just lost mine. He might as well be in a barrel floating down river.

The plane continues deeper and deeper into the blackness, farther away from the surface than I have ever been before.

Instead of going back to the motel, Kenny walked to the Beachcomber bar, where he ordered one martini after the next. For some reason he couldn't get Boner Jones out of his mind. He was such a little goofy kid, so out of control. Soon, Kenny is describing Boner to everyone in the bar. He has to describe everything because maybe they didn't get it the first time. He continues drunkenly talking to whoever is there even when he knows they aren't listening. The bartender pretends to listen as he starts cutting up lemons and limes for the evening crowd that is drifting in. Kenny is not a new customer. He's never been a problem before. This time, however, he is a little louder than usual.

"No one dared call me a fag because I'd already sucked their dick, you see? They were so afraid I would call them out. I was blackmailing the whole football team and the coach never knew. He sent me home for playing dirty. Damn right, I played dirty. I was fighting for my fucking life. I'd go for the knees, step on their hands. I had to. My dad insisted I play center. Shit, I didn't even weigh ninety pounds. But you think my dad cared? Fuck no. When I finally told him I was gay, you know what he said? He said a doctor could fix me. Some one ought to fix you. That's what he said. Some one ought to just cut it off."

Out of nowhere Kenny grabs the bartender's knife.

"You dare me to cut off my finger? Anyone here bet I won't cut off my finger? Come on, Let's put some money on the table."

22

Honeymoon

THE WAVES KEEP on coming one after another . . . the light reflects on the water, turning the gray to silver glints and then back to pewter again, and in between black, as black and cold as the pupil of a shark's eye as it turns helplessly again and again in its tank. Only three months to live. The thought swims back and forth from one side of my skull to the other. I want to escape – to think differently – but I can't.

The idea was to change things by starting over – a second honeymoon. This time, Bobby has promised to act different. But what about me? How am I going to tell him I have the same relentless unloving shark trapped in the fish bowl I am currently calling my head?

According to Kenny, I'm in love with my husband and don't know it, which makes me incredibly stupid, something I'm not buying at the moment. It's Kenny who is the one who is still in love with Bobby, the good-natured blond kid who would go along with anything, not Bobby, the car-dealing pussy hound, who was beginning to get a gut.

Ma was more blunt about my future. Marriage was not about love. As far as I could tell, she married someone she didn't dislike in order to have the great American princess (who now had a shark stuck in her frontal lobe), and on the side, she fucked the owner of the neighborhood casino in order to gamble without a problem. Where is the lesson in that? It's my own fault. I have to stop seeing the black side of everything – back and forth, back and forth.

Meanwhile, Bobby was the ultimate optimist. He didn't want a boring second honeymoon in a hotel paid for by his company, which he fully deserved as the head of sales and company vice-president. He wanted something special, something completely ours and nobody else's. So, he decided to go camping on Ana-cappa, one of the Channel Islands off the coast of California. With all the camping equipment he had accumulated it would be as comfortable as being in a hotel, and we would be alone on an island. Only fifteen people were allowed to stay overnight, and Bobby bought all fifteen tickets. What could be more romantic?

The boat ride over, however, was not romantic. The water looked evil rising in greenish gray slabs, a three-foot chop that made the boat pitch the entire way. Bobby became sea sick, huddling in a corner of the cabin, while the spray hit the window like slaps in the face. I tried the good nurse routine, telling him to go on deck, fresh air was the best antidote, and he could always barf over the edge if it came to that. His eyes looked at me in an agony of shame. Sure, the suggestion of barfing in public was easy for me to say. I was a girl. Girls always fainted, got sick in public, had babies whether they were in the hospital or not. Bobby turned his face to the wall and continued to struggle with his esophagus.

Finally, the island came into view. It didn't look romantic either. Rising out of the gray water, the black rock of Anacappa looked more like a military post than a resort. The only building on the island was a lighthouse, a single white tower above rocks that stuck up like angry teeth tearing the sea into foam. There was no beach, just sheer black cliffs for about two miles around. The only way onto the island was in a little cove where a series of iron stairs and railings were bolted onto the side of the cliff. Okay, I thought, I hate the word "romantic" anyway.

On a little dock at the bottom of the stairs a ranger greeted us, talking as if there were fifteen other campers with us. "Ladies and gentlemen, please stay on the paths. Anacappa is the home and breeding ground for the gray seagull and the chicks are just hatching, so we don't want to disturb them in any way. It's a one-hundred-dollar fine for littering and a five-hundred-dollar fine for any damage done to the birds."

Once we had climbed to the top, dragging our equipment, a field of flowers suspended in the sky rewarded us. The top of Anacappa was ablaze with purple and yellow blossoms mixed with pieces of clouds. Below the sea pounded the rocks like an angry child who couldn't reach the beautiful bowl of flowers above him.

The ranger was right about one thing. This chandelier of flowers that hung so peacefully in the sky was very much occupied. Every foot of the island was fiercely guarded by a mother seagull that screamed at intruders in an attempt to keep them away from her small speckled progeny as they climbed out of their egg and took their first steps on the planet. Nature had given the young gulls a camouflage suit of yellow and gray patches while they waited for their white-feathered wings to grow out. These little polka-dotted pear-shaped squeaking dumdums were programmed to run headlong towards their mother's voice no matter what was approaching, making it impossible to walk at a normal speed without either hitting or stepping on one of the scooting youngsters. So, stumbling single file along one of the many paths that crisscrossed the island, Bobby and I had to constantly watch where we stepped lest one of us squashed the child of the screaming gull before us.

At first it was "oh so cute," but as we marched back and forth to the campsite, dragging all our stuff, it grew less and less cute. The fledglings seemed to wander out of nowhere (maybe they were attracted to shoes). Certainly the idea that they might be stepped on had not yet been formulated in their very tiny brains, nor was it registering on their genetic defense program, which seemed to consist solely of dashing blindly this way and that. The fact that one of us might be responsible for their innocent deaths when they had only just climbed out of the egg was depressing. There were so many of them, and they were everywhere. Instead of a thoughtful and well-equipped camper, Bobby started to feel like a klutz, an awkward Godzilla, and the injustice of it was frustrating him.

We weren't there an hour when the inevitable happened. Bobby stepped on the smallest member of a nearby gull family. Blindly running towards the sound of its mother's screams it had darted under Bobby's new mountain boot and now lay crushed beneath the specially cleated rubber tread. Both Bobby and I stared at Bobby's feet. It looked as if a tank had rolled over the young camouflaged soldier. He didn't have much time to see the world, nor was he ever going to fly like a silver plane out over the ocean.

"We should bury him," I whispered. "We can't afford a fine." I was thinking of something poignant and dramatic when –

"Okay, how is this?" Bobby picked up the little corpse and angrily flung it over the cliff. "Burial at sea."

I was speechless for a second, and so was the whole island, as it listened for the tiny splash of the little soldier's body. Slowly, the calls of the mother gulls started again, only this time they were answered. Rising up from the ocean over the cliff as if they had been launched from an aircraft carrier, a squadron of male gulls flew towards us. The shrieking of irate mothers from the ground intensified, and in response one after another of the male gulls dive-bombed the pair of us until we retreated to our campsite. Under siege we erected our tent and waited for things to blow over. I could swear I had felt little stones hit me from the sky as different gulls soared by, but I decided not to tell Bobby, who was obviously not handling the whole experience very well.

When the sun started going down, turning the hill tops to orange and gold, and the clouds above them to shocking-pink sky fish with lavender underbellies, I ventured outside. Godzilla stayed in his tent, refusing to come. It was the only place he felt safe to move about without creating more injury. One goes camping to make friends with the animals and this massive rejection was depressing for someone who normally picked up other people's litter and was always kind to strays.

Alone, I eagerly made my way to the edge of the island to see the sun peacefully surrender itself to the ocean below. There was nothing peaceful about it. The ocean lay dark and threatening at the bottom of the rocks. I could feel it pulling me as silent shadows came and went under its surface. The mother gulls started screaming at me as if Ma had fallen from the sky and shattered into a million birds. It made me so uncomfortable I couldn't enjoy the sunset, and turning to go back to the tent, I came face to face with the ranger.

"I see you brought a kayak."

"Yes, we thought we would go to the other island." At first I thought he was going to flirt with me, but when he started talking to me, I could feel him change his mind. He could tell I was unhappy, so unhappy he didn't want to hit on me.

"I'm afraid I can't allow you to do that. The Brown Pelicans have chosen that island. They are mating, and if you disturb them they will abandon their nests and never return."

"Why?"

"They are just like that. Once they leave they never come back."

"Even if their young starve to death and die?" He doesn't answer me. His eyes are those of a hunter, they watch me without any emotion. I know his job is to protect me but I feel hunted and nervous. "Everything is mating and blooming here."

"It's spring, ma'am."

"Are there sharks in the water?"

"There are sharks all up and down the southern California coast."

"Is it safe to swim?"

"People do it all the time."

"Great. Thanks for the warning."

"Good night."

Turning on his flashlight, he went back to his cozy bunk in the lighthouse while we struggled with the flowers and the sunset, aware that under the island's beautiful costume, death was crawling and swimming and eating. I knew what he was thinking, that this couple was trouble, not just for him, but for the whole island.

Back in the tent Bobby was fooling with the camping equipment which he had bought at a very posh outback store along with the brand-new mountain-climbing gear and the second-hand cookware he had dragged all the way from Niagara. It was the endless pile of stuff again, and I began to wonder if we really were lying under the stars, high on a black rock in the middle of the ocean, or were we just some camping advertisement surrounded by all our brightly colored equipment. I closed my eyes for a minute trying to imagine where we really were. I wanted to talk to him about Kenny. I know it was the wrong time but if we were going to stay together, there were things I had to know. While I talked, Bobby busied himself trying to get his high-powered camping light to work.

"You know what's funny about all this? We both fell in love with the same man."

"I didn't fall in love with Kenny."

"Okay, Okay. You fell for me, I fell for Kenny, and Kenny fell for you. Between the three of us we were in love for the first time." Bobby moved on to sorting snorkeling equipment.

"Aren't you going to say anything?"

"What's to say?"

"Well, I want to talk about it. I think we should talk."

"I don't." Bobby went back to fixing the camping light again.

"Bobby, I find out that my brother and my husband have – "

"I'd rather talk about us."

"I am talking about us."

"I mean, the present not the past."

"I mean the present too. I mean I have a right to know. What about AIDS?"

"You don't get AIDS from fucking women."

"You can get AIDS from your dentist."

"Yes, but not from women. It's a medical fact."

"You did it with Kenny. What's to stop you from doing it again? Maybe you already have. Maybe you do it all the time. There are married men who go out on their lunch break and – "

What happened next was so quick, it left a blank spot in my mind. Bobby hit me. By the time I realized what he did, he already had his arms around me so I couldn't hit him back.

"I'm sorry. I didn't mean to do that. I want to talk about it. But not here. Not like this . . . with you arguing."

"Get off me."

"Then stop fighting me, stop putting Kenny between us."

I struggled against him, but he held me tight while he continued to talk in a low insistent voice, "You know what I thought after Kenny died? I thought, good, now she'll love me. But even when he was dead you put him between us."

"Let me go, God damn you."

"I'm not going to fuck around, Molly."

"Okay, okay." My shark smashed into the wall full force. "Just do it. Don't tell me about it." My voice was ugly. "Let go."

"Not till you trust me again,"

"Bobby, I can't breathe."

I stopped struggling. I wanted him to hold me, that's what I wanted. That's why we were here. So why was I struggling? "Okay, I trust you." Actually I wanted to kiss and make-up and have fabulous sex. I didn't understand what was going on.

Bobby's arms slid slowly down my body and let me go but he didn't kiss me. Stumbling over the broken camping light, he picked it up and tossed it, "I guess it's not going to work anymore. Anyway, I can't fix it."

Great, I thought, is that some kind of cryptic epitaph for our marriage? I watched him climb into his sleeping bag and followed suit. Both of us laid out in our separate body bags was more like a funeral than a honeymoon. It was so wrong, it was almost funny. The last thing I heard was Bobby's voice in the darkness. It sounded small and far away.

"I hate this island. Tomorrow we're going snorkeling so we don't have to look at this place."

"We'll be the only people in the water. What if there are rip tides?"

"The water turns brown where rip tides are. We can check it out from the cliff."

"I've never snorkeled before."

"Well, I have. Don't worry, Molly, things will look prettier underwater. Now, get some sleep."

"Now, get some sleep" meant we weren't going to fuck. I had screwed up on the first night of our second honeymoon, and Bobby didn't want to talk about it. I should never mention Kenny? I should learn not to argue? I should be more fun in general? I don't know – back and forth, back and forth.

Sleep comes with a dream that was anything but restful. I find myself going downstairs, one after the other, extending forever, endlessly downwards. They are iron stairs like the ones attached to the sheer rock walls of this island. But these stairs are painted white and they are attached to the sides of a gigantic tank, which seems empty. It's big enough for an airplane to turn around in and high as a building. I descend the endless flights of stairs, forty feet, fifty feet, one hundred and twenty feet, down down, until I'm finally at the bottom. In the corner of the tank in only four feet of water my shark hovers belly up. A little white door in the tank wall opens and the ranger enters.

"He's dying. We tried to save him but sharks can't live more than two months in captivity. You should let him go."

"No, I don't want to."

The ranger pulls a lever and the side of the tank starts

to rise, letting the black water of the ocean into the tank.

"No, we'll drown."

"It'll be fine."

23

Underwater

AT SIX AM, feeling more like a prisoner on her way to a firing squad than a honeymooner, I found myself descending the long iron stairs down the black rock of the cliff to the little cove at the bottom. The ocean looked dark and cold, an untrustworthy serpent coiled at the bottom of a pit watching me struggle with my wet suit. It took us an hour to put on the wet suits and other equipment Bobby had more fun buying than using. I felt foolish. I was happy the ranger wasn't there to see us. The ocean serpent coiled and uncoiled excitedly just a few feet away from my left arm. "The water is rougher than it had looked from on top of the cliffs," I said in a small voice. It was one thing to snorkel in the warm beautiful blue waters of the Bahamas but this looked bad. The waters of the Pacific Coast are dark and cold especially on an overcast day.

"Look, Molly, if you don't want to go."

Not wanting to be a spoilsport, I said, "No, I want to go."

"Trust me, Molly."

"Okay." The dock bangs impatiently against the stairs, and the wind slaps the waves noisily, laughing like a hyena. "Okay." I say it again just so he knows I remember last night and I'm going to keep my promise. Looking at the black water, I bite the bullet, and lower myself in. Once my mask slips below the surface everything changes. A door opens in the back of my skull and noiselessly my shark vanishes through it. I am transformed.

It was as if I'd stepped into a movie theater; dark silence enveloped me as a fairy tale world spread before me, a world ruled by silent currents instead of the noisy wind. Ahead was blackness, cold and empty, but looking down I could see an incredible landscape. Imaginary plants moved in long elegant swirls and curls to the timing of violin music. Yet there was no noise, only silence, which made it all seem dreamy and friendly. For the first time since our arrival Bobby and I grinned at each other. We swam down the island coast kicking and holding hands, pointing things out. When we stopped at a little beach of sea lions I was so elated I hugged Bobby, and we started kissing on the beach. I couldn't believe how far we had come and with so little effort. We were almost halfway around the island, so when Bobby suggested swimming all the way around, I agreed, completely forgetting which way the current was moving. Don't all currents only move one way, out to sea?

It wasn't anyone's fault. We were both tricked by this current, a crafty old seductress who played her part well, knowing full well that time was on her side. She swirled the seaweed as if it were one of Salome's veils. The purple grass billowed about her ankles like the royal robes of the dancing queen. A school of tiny silver fish hung suspended, a jeweled veil covering her watery face only to be whisked dramatically away. Coils of golden kelp swayed back and forth as she walked on the shells and starfish that threw themselves at her feet. She danced before us, luring us on, farther and farther, first with this orange Garibaldi and then that unknown neon blue, all the while hiding the roar of the rocks ahead, in the silence of her cape.

The dance continues to the lighthouse, and as we round the point things change. Out of nowhere my mask fills with white foam. I tumble head over heels, banging my shoulder on an enormous rock, which I try to grab on to, but am sucked away. Kicking violently, I try to take advantage of the reverse current to escape colliding with the rock a second time, but another wave shoves me back, this time onto a rock that is slightly out of the water, and I manage to climb onto it.

Two rocks away Bobby is hanging onto what looks like the face of the cliff. His face is badly cut. "We've got to swim through there," he shouts across to me, pointing to a wide gap in the rocks where there is no white water.

All I can see are the rocks; they're jagged, and the waves seem to thunder down on them in comparison to the way they ripple around my rock. But that only means that it is shallower over there. Who knows what the current is like under the smooth water? I stare at the water surging back in against my rock. One can never trust the skin of the water. When it looks silvery and smooth as python skin, underneath the muscles of the current are twisting with vicious power, like steel arms moving under satin sheets.

Bobby yells at me again. "As soon as the wave passes let go and swim." I nod my head. Bobby doesn't look too sure of himself, but there isn't much else we can do.

"The current is going to be against us from now on," I yell back. "We should have been swimming the other way."

Bobby waves his arms in a combination of fury and helplessness. "The waves are getting bigger. Go after this one."

"Okay." Okay? Nothing is okay. My stomach knots as I crouch down. When the wave hits it's like a gunshot at the beginning of a race. The second I push off from the rock every system in my body is screaming SWIM.

I don't feel anything for the first five minutes. Then as the shock leaves my body, I can feel my enemy, fatigue, wrap around my limbs, pulling down my arms and legs. I lock into a pace I think I can hold. From now on it's just a simple refusal to quit. My body is a machine I am prepared to run into the ground. I only have to concentrate on keeping the rhythm steady.

The rocks are definitely behind me, but the current pushes against me like a cement wall. Since no one else is around I start talking to myself, "Great, this is it, the real thing, it's swim or die, and nothing in between. If you stop you'll go out to sea like a stone out of a sling shot." A couple of times I look up to see if Bobby is near, but the two-foot chop in the water prevents me from seeing anything on the surface. All I can see is the black rock of Anacappa looming to my left and a mile away the staircase hanging like a ladder in a dollhouse. The waves slap me in the face forcing a mouthful of water down my throat; putting my head back down I start swimming for the stairs. If I stop to rest, the current in her long green sleeves will pull me back out to the ocean and all the distance I have gained I'll lose as easily as a gambler losing everything on a bad bet. I can hear the current in front of me laughing, her blind eyes covered over by a film as luminous as the inside of a sea shell.

"Okay, shit head, it's only a matter of distance. Even if you could only kick you would still make it." That's what I keep telling myself, aware that my rhythm is slowing down. "So, maybe you picked too fast a pace, and this slower pace is better. I'll keep this pace. Other people have done it. What about the Roman slaves rowing warships to the beat of a drum . . . what about them? The rhythm, you have to keep up the rhythm, never stopping, always kicking, kicking like that drum beat. Off in the distance I could hear it. Niagara softly pounding in my neck until the sound fills my head, its force pumps through my body, unaware that my arms ache or that my legs can't keep track of how fast I'm kicking.

The current let go, her long green sleeves parting with every stroke I took until something large and gray passed underneath me, making me break pace. I didn't need trouble with fish now. Or was my sister shark here? The thought terrified me. A scuba diving story replayed in my brain at high speed; it came like a cannon ball out of nowhere, knocking the diver over, and vanished as silently as it came. Looking behind him the diver saw his partner was sprouting dark clouds from his armless socket, but before he could do anything the shark was back with the force of a locomotive only this time it caught his partner's tank in its mouth, saving the story-teller. That image of the shark traveling so fast from so far away like a guided missile tracking blood seized my mind and my rhythm broke.

Another larger thing moves past me, and my terror escalates to joy. It looks like plastic. I'm sure it's plastic. I'm not going to look back, but garbage means civiliz-ation. Then over to my left something brown and white moves, a candy wrapper, and over there is a potato chip bag caught under a rock. I have to be near the cove. Picking my head up I see the stairs, not small and far away, but big and nearby.

Limping into the protected waters of the cove, I half float and half kick myself to the stairs. At first I'm too tired to climb up. I just hang there like a fish on a hook, shamelessly pissing into my wet suit. The only bad part of this scenario was that I was alone. I climbed up the first bunch of stairs. I couldn't see Bobby anywhere. I climbed more stairs. Bobby wasn't anywhere in sight. I climbed to where I could see the entire ocean, but Bobby didn't seem to be in that ocean, or at least not on the surface of it.

The thought of the treacherous current letting me go and at the same time pulling Bobby underwater by the ankles, and slamming him against the rocks again and again, started throbbing in my head. No longer the enchantress, the bitch current had now become the conqueror, dragging her victim on the ground for all the fish to see. Silently they watch as their mistress rolls him along the ocean floor, tearing his tattered wet suit from off his white body, and kicking his corpse into the ocean where, finally naked, he is hers. She snaps off his head and presses her lips against his mouth in the kiss that is her victory. The dance is over. And dinner is served to the staring fish who approach cautiously for tentative bites, not really sure if they like their mistress's choice of food today.

I felt utterly exhausted and sick, but through my clenched teeth I was going to have to swallow a lethal dose of guilt. It was beginning to look like I had saved my own life, and in the process left my husband to die. Wasn't it the scuba diver's rule that you never leave your partner? Sure, I was a good swimmer, but I don't remember if Bobby was. I don't remember Bobby swimming in the river with us. I was too busy thinking about my own performance to realize I had never really seen him swim, not heavy-duty laps in a pool, never. The idea that he knew he couldn't make it but wanted me to go on without him was just too corny. I couldn't think of it.

Scrambling all the way to the top of the stairs, I looked around. There was a metal telescope on the rail, the kind you put a quarter in to see the sights, but I didn't have a quarter. Going up to the telescope I put my eyes to it anyway, and it worked. Scanning the ocean from the cove to the point, I saw nothing. Then I looked farther out to sea, praying that I wouldn't find him so far from land. Very far out I saw the tour boat on its way over, and remembering how unconsciously they had plowed their way here, I thought what if they run him over? Holding onto the rail, I shut my eyes. My last conversation with God didn't go very well, but I didn't know what else to do. "Dear God, make him be alive. I'll do anything. Anything, do you hear?" I opened my eyes. Nothing. The empty gray sea stared back at me.

The empty sky hung above me. Empty, everything was empty.

Run, run back down the stairs. Bobby didn't make it, and I did . . . it was becoming a reality. The only thing to do was go back and get him. At the bottom of the cove the water stared back at me, its cold coils waiting to pull me down. Death was right there, in the cove, just under the surface of the water, swimming back and forth, back and forth. What do we do? Ma, you forgot to tell me. My brain started to flatline. I sank down on the dock. I couldn't make myself jump in. I was too weak to struggle against the current again, maybe in a movie, but not in real life. I needed help . . . the ranger.

Back up the stairs I went, this time pretty much on all fours with my hands gripping the top steps like a monkey. My wet suit wasn't helping me climb these stairs, but there was no time to take it off. As I scrambled up the now very familiar stairs I felt the ranger watching me from the top. Had he come out to laugh at me? He probably had never seen a tourist put on a wet suit and run up and down the stairs before. Some new insane exercise that was in fashion.

"Where is your husband?"

"I don't know," I suddenly felt stupid. Not everyone loses a husband on their honeymoon. "We swam around the island and at the point the current was too strong – " I didn't bother finishing.

"Always swim against the current so on your way back when you are tired the current is with you."

"Well, we didn't, and now Bobby is missing. I can't see him." I was having trouble talking. "I can't swim back there to find him. I can't deal with this, I mean I don't know how. A boat, maybe. You must have a boat?" The ranger wasn't listening to me so I caught my hysterical voice and smothered it on the other side of my teeth with the rest of my tongue. Watching the ranger's eyes scan the water I thought of a radar screen, and wondered if he was an android who had been planted out here.

"The wet suit should keep him floating. Did he have one on?"

"Yes."

The gulls were quiet.

"How long will it keep him floating?" Was Bobby floating in the ocean now, wondering what he was going to eat for lunch?

"I can tell the tour boat to pick him up if he's out there."

Poor Bobby, I thought, not only had his wife outswum him, but he would have to endure the public humiliation of being rescued by the tour boat. "Where is he? Do you see him?"

"No, but he's out there somewhere. You must be a good swimmer. We've lost people in that current."

"I know, it's my fault for not staying with him."

"I didn't say that," he said in a softer voice. "I said you're a good swimmer."

I left the ranger staring at the empty sea, and started down the endless stairs again, back and forth, back and forth. Stop it . . . this isn't going to be the fucking end. It couldn't be, I didn't make that call to Kenny yet. I would be okay because I wouldn't have to swim. The current would carry me right back to Bobby who I'm sure never left his rock. And the ranger would call the tour boat and, to our embarrassment, all the tourists would applaud and cheer because it was the first rescue mission they'd ever been on. The whole episode would turn into one of those family stories our kids wanted to hear over and over, how mommy rescued daddy, while Uncle Kenny rolled his eyes and Grandma May . . . As I stepped onto the dock, my happy story evaporated, leaving me feeling small and alone.

I wondered if this was what a real hero felt like, terrible. I didn't want to die. I didn't even want to get wet. Looking at the water, I felt cold. My body felt cold and numb. It was just as well because what lay before me wasn't going to be pleasant. I knew I couldn't swim much more, but I was on automatic. I had to rescue Bobby even if I was too late. I slid off the dock. It was more of a fall than a jump. A weight around my neck and shoulders vanished as the sea closed over my head.

I look around. It's black ahead, not the black of a starless night that you want to fly up into, but the dead color of a wall that has been painted black. Swimming into it, my dorsal fin cuts the surface like a knife. Riding the current easily, I feel no need to surface for air. My neck opens in gill formation and my teeth grow in long pointed rows. This will be my home, the black waters of the Channel Islands, swimming back and forth, back and forth, looking for Bobby's body, looking for a field of crimson roses to lie down in. My next reincarnation is here in this sunless world, looking for bodies as my father had done along the river. At the edge of the cove the water turned suddenly cold.